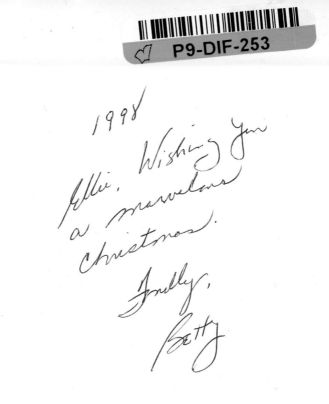

1998

Ellie, Wishing you
a marvelous
Christmas.

Fondly,

Betty

Also by Richard Paul Evans

THE CHRISTMAS BOX

TIMEPIECE

RICHARD PAUL EVANS

SIMON & SCHUSTER

SIMON & SCHUSTER
Rockefeller Center
1230 Avenue of the Americas
New York, NY 10020

SIMON & SCHUSTER and colophon are registered trademarks
of Simon & Schuster Inc.

Designed by Pei Loi Koay

Printed in Great Britain

1 3 5 7 9 10 8 6 4 2

Library of Congress Cataloging-in-Publication Data
Evans, Richard Paul.
Timepiece / Richard Paul Evans.
p. cm.
I. Title.
PS3555.V259T56 1996
813'.54—dc20 96-6971
CIP
ISBN 0-684-81576-1

ACKNOWLEDGMENTS

t is a pleasure to express my appreciation and love to the following.

My wife, Keri. Jenna, Allyson-Danica, and Abigail, for sharing their Dad with the world.

My two Lauries: Laurie Liss, I could not have asked for a better agent or friend; and my editor, Laurie Chittenden, thank you for coming, thank you for making *Timepiece* better. Carolyn Reidy, MaryAnn Naples, and all my friends at S&S who believed we could make history with *The Christmas Box* and then did. Isolde Sauer and Beth Greenfeld for additional editing assistance. Mary

Schuck. William Barfus, Janet Bernice, and the gracious assistance of the Utah Historical Society. Ann Deneris. Chris Harding and Beth Polson, for believing in signs. My brother Mark for everything. Evan Twede for friendship, perspective, and TGI Friday's. Mary Kay Lazarus and Elaine Pine-Peterson. The Beutlers: Bill, Cora, and Scott. Mike Hurst. John Stringham, who, in many ways, made this book possible. Senator Robert F. Bennett and Michael Tullis. Mayor Deedee Coradini and Governor Mike Leavitt for inviting the world to Salt Lake City. SLC Cemetery Sexton Paul Byron. My parents, David and June Evans, for their work with The Christmas Box Foundation, and, of course, everything else. Ortho and Jared Fairbanks who sculpted the angel. Cathi Lammert of SHARE Pregnancy and Infant Loss Support, Inc.

And to the dreamers who are bound with golden bracelets—my brother, Barry J. Evans, Celeste Edmunds, Shelli Holmes, and Michele Feldt. Thank you for believing.

SHARE: Pregnancy and Infant Loss Support, Inc., offers support to parents who have lost a baby through miscarriage, stillbirth, or early infant death. For more information please call: 1-800-821-6819.

To my wife, Keri,

and to my mother,

June.

Both of whom have given me life.

CONTENTS

Contents

The only promise of childhood is that it will end.

I find myself astonished at mankind's persistent yet vain attempts to escape the certainty of oblivion; expressed in nothing less than the ancient pyramids and by nothing more than a stick in a child's hand, etching a name into a freshly poured sidewalk. To leave our mark in the unset concrete of time—something to say we existed.

Perhaps this is what drives our species to diaries, that some unborn generation may know we once loved, hated, worried, and laughed. And what is there to this? Maybe nothing more than poetic gesture, for diaries die with their authors—or so I once believed. I have learned there is more to the exercise. For as we chronicle our lives and the circumstances that surround them, our perspectives and stretching rationales, what lies before us is our own reflection. It is the glance in the mirror that is of value. These are my words on the matter and I leave it at this—if we write but one book in life, let it be our autobiography.

◆

The most valuable of the keepsakes left in the attic of the Parkin mansion were thought worthless by the auctioneers of the estate. They were the leather-bound diaries of David Parkin. A lifetime of hopes and dreams, thought of no significance by those who value only what could bring cash at an auction block. The diaries came into my possession shortly after we took leave of the mansion, and it was within the pages of David's diary that I found the meaning of MaryAnne Parkin's last request. For this reason, I have shared his words throughout my narrative—for without them, the story would be incomplete.

And if it is nothing more than poetic gesture, then still I am justified.

For poetry, like life, is its own justification.

CHAPTER ONE

The Grandfather's Clock

"Of all, clockmakers and morticians should bear the keenest sense of priority—their lives daily spent in observance of the unflagging procession of time . . . and the end thereof."

DAVID PARKIN'S DIARY. JANUARY 3, 1901

hen I was a boy, I lived in horror of a clock—a dark and foreboding specter that towered twice my height in the hardwood hallway of my childhood home and even larger in my imagination.

It was a mahogany clock, its hood rising in two wooden cues that curled like horns on a devil's head. It had a brass-embossed face, black, serpentine hands, and a flat, saucer-sized pendulum.

To this day, I can recall the simple and proud incantations of its metallic chime. At my youthful insistence, and to my father's dismay, the strike silent was never employed, which meant the clock chimed every fifteen minutes, night and day.

I believed then that this clock had a soul—a belief not much diminished through age or accumulated experience. This species of clock was properly called a longcase clock, until a popular music hall song of the nineteenth century immortalized one of its ilk and forever changed the name. The song was titled "My Grandfather's Clock," and during my childhood, more than a half century after the song was written, it was still a popular children's tune. By the age of five, I had memorized the song's lyrics.

> *My grandfather's clock was too large for the shelf,*
> *so it stood ninety years on the floor,*
> *It was taller by half than the old man himself,*
> *tho' it weighed not a penny-weight more.*
> *It was bought on the morn of the day that he was born,*
> *and was always his treasure and pride,*
> *But it stopp'd short never to go again*
> *when the old man died.*

My fear of the hallway clock had its roots in the song's final refrain.

> *But it stopp'd short never to go again*
> *when the old man died.*

When I was young, my mother was sickly and often bedridden with ailments I could neither pronounce nor comprehend. With the reasoning and imagination of childhood, I came to believe that if the clock stopped, my mother would die.

Often, as I played alone in our quiet house after my brothers had left for school, I would suddenly feel my heart grasped by the hand of panic and I would run to my mother's darkened bedroom. Peering through the doorway, I would wait for the rise and fall of her chest, or the first audible gasp of her breath. Sometimes, if she had had an especially bad day, I would lie awake at night listening for the clock's quarter-hour chime. Twice I ventured downstairs to the feared oracle to see if its pendulum was still alive.

To my young mind, the clock's most demonic feature was the hand-painted moon wheel set above its face in the clock's arch. Mystically, the wheel turned with the waning moon, giving the clock a wizardry that, as a child, transfixed and mystified me as if it somehow knew the mysterious workings of the universe. And the mind of God.

It is my experience that all childhoods have ghosts.

♦

Tonight, just outside my den stands a similar grandfather's clock—one of the few antiques my wife and I received from MaryAnne Parkin, a kind widow we shared a home with for a short while before her death nearly nineteen years ago. The clock had been a gift to her on her wedding day from her husband, David, and during our stay in the mansion it occupied the west wall of the marble-floored foyer.

David Parkin had been a wealthy Salt Lake City businessman and a collector of rare antiquities. Before his death, in 1934, he had accumulated an immense collection of rare furniture, Bibles, and, most of all, clocks. Time-marking devices of all kinds—from porcelain-encased pocket watches to hewn-stone sundials filled the Parkin home. Of his vast collection of timekeepers, the grandfather's clock, which now stands outside my doorway, was the most valuable—a marvel of nineteenth-century art and engineering and the trophy of David's collection. Even still, there was one timepiece that he held in greater esteem. One that he, and MaryAnne, cherished above all: a beautiful rose-gold wristwatch.

Only eleven days before her death, MaryAnne Parkin had bequeathed the timepiece to my keeping.

"The day before you give Jenna away," she had said, her hands and voice trembling as she handed me the heirloom, "give this to her for the gift."

I was puzzled by her choice of words.

"Her wedding gift?" I asked.

She shook her head and I recognized her characteristic vagueness. She looked at me sadly, then forced a fragile smile. "You will know what I mean."

I wondered if she really believed that I would or had merely given the assurance for her own consolation.

It had been nineteen winters since Keri, Jenna, and I had shared the mansion with the kindly widow, and though I had often considered her words, their meaning eluded me still. It haunted me that I had missed something that she, who understood life so well, regarded with such gravity.

Tonight, upstairs in her bedroom, my daughter Jenna, now a young woman of twenty-two, is engaged in the last-minute chores of a bride-to-be. In the morning, I will give her hand to another man. A wave of melancholy washed over me as I thought of the place she would leave vacant in our home and in my heart.

The gift? What in the curriculum of fatherhood had I failed to learn?

I leaned back in my chair and admired the exquisite heirloom. MaryAnne had received the watch in 1918 and, even then, it was already old: crafted in a time when craftsmanship was akin to religion—before the soulless reproductions of today's mass-market assembly.

The timepiece was set in a finely polished rose-gold encasement. It had a perfectly round face with tiny numerals etched beneath a delicate, raised crystal. On each side of the face, intricately carved in gold, were scallopshell-shaped clasps connecting the casing to a matching rose-gold scissor watchband. I have never before, or since, seen a timepiece so beautiful.

From the dark hallway outside my den, the quarter-hour chime of the grandfather's clock disrupted my thoughts—as if beckoning for equal attention.

The massive clock had always been a curiosity to

me. When we had first moved into the Parkin mansion, it sat idle in the upstairs parlor. On one occasion, I asked MaryAnne why she didn't have the clock repaired.

"Because," she replied, "it isn't broken."

◆

Treasured as it is, the clock has always seemed out of place in our home, like a relic of another age—a prop left behind after the players had finished their lines and taken their exits. In one of those exits is the tale of David and MaryAnne Parkin. And so, too, the riddle of the timepiece.

CHAPTER TWO

Mary Anne

Salt Lake City, 1908

"A young woman came to my office today to apply for employment. She is a rather handsome woman, and, though simply dressed, exuded both warmth and grace, a pleasant diversion from the society women I too frequently encounter who exhibit the cold refinement of a sterling tea service. I proceeded to acquaint myself with her, offend her, and hire her all in the course of one half hour. Her name is MaryAnne Chandler and she is an Englishwoman.

"There is a curious chemistry between us."

DAVID PARKIN'S DIARY. APRIL 16, 1908

lectric sparks fell like fireworks from the suspended cables of a trolley car, as the brash clangor of its bell pierced the bustle of the wintry Salt Lake

City streets. At its passing, MaryAnne glanced across the snow and the mud-churned road, lifted her skirt above her ankles, and crossed the street, stepping between the surreys and traps that lined the opposite stretch of the cement walk. Near the center of the block, she entered a doorway marked in arched, gold-leafed letters: PARKIN MACHINERY Cº. OFFICE.

As she pulled the door shut behind herself, the chill sounds of winter dissolved into the cacophony of human industry. Brushing the snow from her shoulders, she glanced around the enormous room.

Its high ceiling was upheld by dark wooden Corinthian columns from which projected the brass fittings of gaslights. Maplewood desks lined the hardwood floor, each with a small rug delineating the employee's work space.

An oak railing separated the work floor from the entryway, and the man who occupied the desk nearest the entrance acknowledged MaryAnne with clerklike nonchalance. He was a balding man, attired in a wool suit and vest with a gold chain spanning his ample girth.

"I am here to see Mr. Parkin about a secretarial situation," MaryAnne announced. She pulled the kerchief back from her hair, revealing a gentle complexion and high, shapely cheekbones. Her beauty piqued the clerk's interest.

"Have you an appointment with Mr. Parkin?"

"Yes. He is expecting me at nine. I am a few minutes early."

Without explanation, the clerk stepped away from his desk and disappeared through an oak doorway near the back of the spacious room. A few minutes later he returned, followed by another individual, a well-groomed young man in his early thirties.

The man had a pleasant face with strong but not overbearing features. He was of medium height and well proportioned, with dark, coffee-colored hair, which had been parted and brushed back in the latest continental style. His eyes were azure blue and alive with interest in all that moved about him. He wore no jacket, revealing the pleated front of his wing-collared shirt and the garters that held his sleeves. He carried himself casually, yet with a confidence that bespoke his importance with the firm.

"Miss Chandler?"

"Yes."

He extended his hand. "Thank you for coming. If you will please follow me," he said, motioning to the door he had just emerged from. MaryAnne followed him through the doorway, then down an oak-paneled corridor to a staircase. She stopped her escort at the foot of the stairs.

"Sir, if I may inquire . . . ?"

He turned and faced her. "Yes. Of course."

"When I address Mr. Parkin, shall I call him 'Mr. Parkin' or 'sir'?"

The young man considered the question. "He likes to be called 'Your Majesty.'"

MaryAnne was dumbstruck.

"I am joking, Miss Chandler. I don't suppose it matters at all what you call him."

"I am not seeking to flatter him. I am just grateful to be able to meet with someone as prominent as Mr. Parkin. I hope to make a favorable impression."

"I am certain that you will do just that."

"Why so?"

"Because I am David Parkin."

MaryAnne flushed. She covered her mouth with her hand. "You are so young to . . ."

". . . Be a millionaire?"

MaryAnne turned a brighter shade of crimson, at which David chuckled. "I am sorry, Miss Chandler, I should have introduced myself properly. Please come up to my office."

They climbed the stairway to the second level and entered a corner office overlooking Second South and Main Street. The office was large and the cherrywood cabinets and shelves that lined the walls were cluttered with books and a score of mantel clocks, which were used as bookends and adornment. No fewer than a dozen other clocks—free standing cabinet or wag-on-the-wall clocks—garnished the room as well. Outside of a clock shop, MaryAnne had never seen such a congregation. They ticked loudly and she wondered how anyone could think in such a place.

In the center of the room was a beautiful hand-carved mahogany desk with a gold-embossed leather writing surface dyed in rich green and umber hues. To its side was a Dictaphone table with a large battery box underneath.

"May I assist you with your coat?" David offered, helping to slip the wet garment from her shoulders.

"Thank you."

MaryAnne settled into a wooden chair, straightened her dress and lay her hands in her lap, while David returned to his desk.

"You have many clocks."

He smiled pleasantly. "I collect them. At the top of the hour, there is quite a racket."

MaryAnne smiled. "I would think so."

David sat down at his desk. "Your accent betrays you. You are from England, are you not?"

She nodded.

"What part of England?"

"A borough of London. Camden Town."

"I was through there a few summers back. Just outside of Regent's Park. I occasionally spend time in England at the auctions."

She smiled. "I have fond memories of Regent's Park."

David leaned forward in his chair. "Your letter said that you are skilled in secretarial work."

"Yes. I have three years' experience on the typewriter, both a Hammond and a Remington. I know Pitman's shorthand and am a member of the Phonetic Society. I have used a Dictaphone," she replied, pointing to the heavy table a few feet from his desk. "An Edison model like this one. I have also kept a register for six months." Then, looking up at a row of clocks, she added, "And I am very punctual."

David smiled at her reference to the clocks.

MaryAnne reached into her purse and brought out a bundle of papers. "I brought letters."

David accepted the papers. "Where did you acquire your skills, Miss Chandler?"

"I worked with Marley and Sons Glaziers as Mr. Marley's assistant. When Mr. Marley took ill, I was given leave. He passed on shortly afterward. Then I went to work at Walker's stationery shop on Main Street. I typed invoices and recorded receipts. The shop closed on account of the death of Mr. Walker."

"This is not a good omen, Miss Chandler. Do all your employers release you through such somber means?"

"I prefer to think that they would rather die than release me."

David smiled at her quick reply. "So it would seem. How much did the position pay?"

She swallowed nervously. "I require twelve dollars a week."

David looked back down at her letters. "You were only two weeks at your last employment." He paused, inviting response.

She hesitated. "I could not meet my supervisor's expectations."

David was surprised by her honesty. "Exactly what was it that you found so challenging?"

"I would rather not say."

"I appreciate your hesitation, Miss Chandler, but if I am to hire you in good faith, it is quite essential that I know your limitations."

"Yes," she relented. She turned from her interrogator and took a deep breath. "Sitting on his lap."

David cocked his head.

MaryAnne blushed. "Sitting on his lap," she repeated. "My supervisor wanted me to sit on his lap."

"Oh," David replied. "You will find none of that in this office." He hurriedly changed the subject. "How is it that you came to live in Salt Lake City? It is not a place you accidentally arrive at."

"My father came from England in the hope of capitalizing on what was left of the gold rush. When we arrived at Ellis island, he heard that California was either panned out or the big finds were controlled by large interests, but that there had recently been a large silver strike in Salt Lake City. So my father brought his family out to settle. I was only seven years old at the time."

"Your father came to mine?"

"No. To sell goods to the miners. He said it is easier to pan gold from a purse than a river."

"A wise man, your father. I have never seen so many fools work so hard for easy money and end up with so little of it. How did he fare in the business?"

"Unfortunately, my father was not of good health. He died shortly after our arrival in the valley. The West is not an easy place for a man used to the comfortable life of nobility."

"Your father was a nobleman?"

"My father was the second son of a baron."

David studied her carefully, resting his chin on his hands. "And that makes you . . ."

"It makes me nothing, as I am an American."

David nodded. "It is just as well," he said. He leaned back, lacing his fingers behind his head. "A title is much too troublesome and high-minded."

MaryAnne glared back, certain that she or, at the very least, her ancestors had been offended. "Whatever do you mean?"

"I believe Your Grace was saying," David said, adopting an exaggerated British accent. "My Most Reverend, Most Noble, Right Honorable, Venerable, Duke, Duchess, Squire, Lord, Lady, Baron, Baroness, Viscount, Marquess, Earl." He breathed out in feigned exasperation. "It is a business in itself and all too tiresome."

"You mock me!"

David waved a hand. "No. No. I am merely amused by the show."

MaryAnne sat back, her arms folded defensively across her chest. "America has its castes."

"True. But in America they are for sale."

MaryAnne glowered, then suddenly stood up, brushing down her skirt as she rose. "I think I shall go now, Mr. Parkin."

Her response surprised him and the smile left David's face.

"I have offended you."

"Not in the least," she replied, raising her chin indignantly.

"No, I have. I am sorry. Please don't go."

She said nothing.

"I apologize, Miss Chandler. I did not mean to be offensive. Attribute my rudeness to my crass upbringing as an American. Surely you cannot begrudge me of that."

"Pity you, perhaps."

"Touché," David said, grinning.

She retrieved her coat from the pole and put it on. David walked over to the doorway. "MaryAnne, I should like to work together. I will pay you eighteen dollars a week. If you choose to accept, you may begin immediately."

MaryAnne lifted her chin proudly, retaining an air of indignation. "I will see you Monday morning at five minutes to eight, Mr. Parkin."

David grinned. "It will be a pleasure, Miss Chandler."

CHAPTER THREE

David

"My new secretary manifests a peculiar confederation of English ritual and American sensibility. I enjoy her company, though she seems of a rather serious nature and I wish she were not so formal."

DAVID PARKIN'S DIARY. APRIL 29,1908

n hour after the close of the business week, Gibbs, the company's head clerk, lumbered up the stairway sporting a tumbler in each chubby fist. When he reached David's office, he was breathing heavily. He set the glasses on the desk and announced, "I brought you some port."

David was standing behind his desk thumbing through a leather-bound manual. He brought the volume to his desk and sat down.

"Ah, you are well trained, Gibbs. Or at least opportunistic. Thank you." He bowed back over the book.

Gibbs took a chair in front of the desk and claimed one of the drinks as his own. "The Salisbury mine is now in possession of a new ore crusher and our account runneth over."

"Well done, Gibbs. It is a strong year."

"They have all been strong years." Gibbs looked around the room. "Your girl is gone?"

"MaryAnne? Yes, she has left for the day."

"You have not said much of her."

David continued reading, acknowledging the observation with only a nod.

"Is she capable?"

David looked up from his register. "She is wonderful. In fact, I am growing quite fond of her."

Gibbs pushed back in his chair. "Fond? Why so?"

David closed the book. "She is a curiosity to me. She has the work ethic of a farm wife and the refinement of the well-bred." He took a drink. "Only better, for it is not an acquired grace, but a natural refinement."

"Refinement?" Gibbs laughed. "Wasted on the likes of you."

David grinned. "No doubt." He set down his tumbler. "Still, they use the pig to find truffle."

"A fitting analogy, I might say."

"You might not," David countered.

Gibbs laughed. "Her apparel is common enough."

"Mark me. She is a poor woman with nobility hidden beneath rags."

"And you a rich man with the common touch. How incongruous."

"How perfect."

"How so?"

David leaned back in his chair. "Two oddities make a normality. It works in mathematics, as in life."

"You are still just talking about a secretary?" Gibbs asked sardonically.

David studied his associate's expression with consternation.

"I have said more than I ought and you have clearly heard more than I have said." He lifted his glass to the light. "Is there much talk among the typists?"

"Some. They like a scandal and if they cannot find one, they invent one."

"Then I suppose I am doing them a service of sorts."

He leaned back over his register. "Still, I wish she were not so formal."

Just then, the first of the mantel clocks struck the seventh hour, immediately followed by a chorus of bells, gongs, and chimes, all counting out the hour in a different voice. Gibbs, accustomed to the hourly pandemonium, waited for it to settle before continuing. "I think you are asking for trouble, David. Love and business do not mix well."

"Gibbs, you surprise me. What do you know of love?"

The man licked the rim of his glass, then set it down on the desk. "Only that it is the worm that conceals the hook."

"You are cynical."

"And you are not?"

David frowned. "I should be."

Gibbs nodded knowingly. He had grown up with David in the California mining town of Grass Valley and knew of what David spoke. David's mother had abandoned him as a child and stolen from him as an adult.

Rosalyn "Rose" King, a music hall singer of mediocre ability, had married David's father, Jesse Parkin, believing he would someday strike the mother lode. Ten years later the two had managed to produce only a son and a miserly shaft mine called the Eureka.

The year David turned six, Rose abandoned the Midas dream and left everything, including David, behind. It wasn't until the lonely and celebrationless Christmas day of that year that David accepted that his mother wasn't coming back.

Thirteen years to the month of her departure, the Eureka lived up to its name. It was to be one of the largest gold strikes in California history.

Jesse ceded the mine to his son's care, built a sixteen-hundred-acre ranch in Santa Rosa, and settled about the life of a Western Gentleman. Not two years later, Jesse was thrown from a horse and died instantly of a broken neck.

Gibbs accompanied David as he buried his father in the foothills of Mount Saint Helena. David mourned greatly.

The following spring, David received a letter from a mother he no longer knew. Rose had come West to Salt Lake City and learning of her husband's fortune and recent demise, inquired into the will. Learning that David was the sole heir and not yet married, she invited him to come and live with her, with the urgent request that he send money ahead.

Against Gibbs's advice, David sold the mine. In a day when the average annual income was scarcely more than a thousand dollars, the Eureka fetched two million.

David wired twenty-five thousand dollars to his mother and purchased, sight unseen, an elaborate Salt Lake City mansion for them to reside in.

By the time he and Gibbs arrived in the Salt Lake Valley in spring of 1897, his mother had taken the money and moved to Chicago with a man she had met only three weeks previously, leaving only a penned regret that forever lies pressed between the pages of David's journal.

As powerful as David had become financially, in matters of the heart he was vulnerable and Gibbs brooded over him, protecting him from those who sought financial gain through romantic liaison. This role gave Gibbs no pleasure, however, for he knew his friend's loneliness. Despite David's unhappy experience, he desired the companionship marriage brings, but was not sure how to proceed, viewing women much as the novice card player who understands the rules, but not how the game is really played.

◆

David finished his drink, then set it down in front of him as his friend studied him sadly. Gibbs gathered the empty glasses and stood to leave. "Still, she is quite pretty."

After a moment, David looked up. "Yes. Quite."

CHAPTER FOUR

Lawrence

"The first mechanical clock was invented in the year A.D. 979 in Kaifeng, China. Commissioned by the boy emperor for the purpose of astrological fortune-telling, the clock took eight years to construct and weighed more than two tons. Though of monstrous dimensions, the device was remarkably efficient, striking a gong every fourteen minutes and twenty-four seconds, nearly identical to our modern-day standard, at the same time turning massive rings designed to replicate the celestial movements of the three luminaries: the sun, the moon, and selected stars, all of which were crucial to Chinese astrological divination.

"When the Tartars invaded China in 1108, they plundered the capital city and after disassembling the massive clock, carted it back to their own lands. Unable to put the precision piece back together, they melted it down for swords."

NOTE IN DAVID PARKIN'S DIARY

MaryAnne knocked gently at David's door, then opened it enough to peer in. "Mr. Parkin, you have a visitor."

David glanced up. "Who is it?"

"He would not give his name. He says he is a close friend."

"I am not expecting anyone. What does he look like?"

"He is an older gentleman . . ."

David shrugged.

". . . and he is a Negro."

"A Negro? I do not want to see any Negroes."

"I am sorry, sir. He said he was a close friend."

Just then, the man appeared behind MaryAnne. He was a large man, dressed as a soldier in a navy cotton shirt and tan pants with a leather bullet belt clasped to a silver cavalry buckle. He smiled at David. "David, you givin' this nice lady a bad time."

David grinned. "I could not resist. Come in, Lawrence."

Surprised, MaryAnne stepped back and pulled open the door for him to enter.

"Sorry, ma'am. It's David's sense of humor."

"Or lack of," she replied.

Lawrence laughed jovially. "I like you, ma'am. Who is this lady, David?"

"Lawrence, meet Miss MaryAnne Chandler. She is my new secretary. Miss Chandler, this is Lawrence. He is the godfather to most of the clocks you see in this room."

"It is a pleasure meeting you, sir."

Lawrence bowed. "It's my pleasure, ma'am."

"Gentlemen, if I may be excused."

David nodded and MaryAnne stepped away, shutting the door behind her.

"Where's Miss Karen?" Lawrence asked.

"It has been a while since you have been around. Her mother took ill and she went back to Georgia."

"She was a nice gal."

"Yes. She did not think much of Negroes, though."

"Her upbringin'," Lawrence said in her defense.

"You are kinder than you ought to be," David said, reclining in his chair. "What have you brought to show me?"

Lawrence lifted a gold pocket watch by its bob and

handed it to David, who examined it carefully, then held it out at arm's length. "Look at that," he said beneath his breath.

"It's a fine piece. Maybe the finest I seen. French made. Never even been engraved. Belonged to a Mr. Nathaniel Kearns."

"Gold plate?"

"Solid."

"How much does Kearns want for it?"

"Mr. Kearns don't want nothin'. He's dead. The auctioneers askin' seventy-five dollars."

"Is it worth it?"

"Sixty-seven dollars, I'd say."

"I will purchase it," David decided. "For sixty-seven." He stood up. "Would you care for something to drink?" He pulled a crystal decanter from a cabinet against the west wall.

"Shore I would."

David poured Lawrence a shot glass of rum. Lawrence took the glass, then leaned back while David walked back to his chair.

"How long this MaryAnne worked for you?"

"About six weeks." The corners of his mouth rose in a vague smile. "She is rather special."

"I can see that," he said. "Called me 'suh'."

David nodded, then glanced over to the door to be certain it was closed. "I have a question for you, Lawrence."

Lawrence looked up intently over his glass.

"What do you think of me marrying?"

"You, David?"

"What would you say to that?"

"Now why you askin' me? I ain't ever been married."

"I value your opinion. You are a good judge of character."

Lawrence fidgeted uncomfortably.

"Come now, Lawrence. Speak freely."

Lawrence frowned. "It's my way of thinkin' that some folk shouldn' get themselves married."

David grinned. "Some folk? Folk like me?"

"I'm jus' sayin' someone shouldn' take a perfectly good life and go marryin' it. Seen it happen my whole life, someone has the good life. Plenty to eat. Plenty of time to jus' do nuthin', then a woman comes 'long and ruins it all."

David began to laugh. "Lawrence, you have a clarity of thought I envy."

"There someone you be thinkin' 'bout?"

"Yes. But I think she would be rather astonished to know of my intentions."

Lawrence glanced back toward the door and smiled knowingly.

"You do have a clarity of thought, my friend," David said.

Lawrence stood up. "Well, I best be off so you can be 'bout your business." His face stretched into a bright smile. "Whatever that business may be."

David grinned. "Thank you for bringing the time-piece by, Lawrence. I will come by this afternoon with the payment."

Lawrence stopped at the door. "Ain't no woman goin' to like all those clocks 'round her house."

"The right one will."

Lawrence opened the door and looked out at MaryAnne, who glanced up and smiled at him. He turned back toward David, who was examining his new timepiece. "You have an eye for finer things."

"So do you, Lawrence. So do you."

◆

Lawrence was a novelty in his neighborhood and the children of his street would wait patiently for his daily, slow-paced pilgrimage to the Brigham Street market, then scatter like birds at his appearance. No child could visit the area without hearing the boast from the indigenous children, "We got a Negro in our neighbor-hood."

His home was a ramshackle hut built behind a large brick cannery, and all in the neighborhood knew of its existence, despite the fact that it was well secluded and Lawrence was as inconspicuous as his skin allowed him to be.

Lawrence's last name was Flake, taken from the slave owners who had purchased his mother in eastern Louisiana in 1834. He had seen war twice, once in the South, and once in Cuba, and had grown old in the military, his black hair dusted silver with age.

He was tall, six foot, and broad-shouldered, and though he had a thick, powerful neck, his head hung slightly forward, a manifestation of a life of deference. His skin was patched and uneven from exposure to the elements, but his eyes were clear and quiet and said all that society would not allow spoken.

He walked with a limp, which increased with his age. The adult spectators of his daily march called it a Negro shuffle, ignorant of the Spanish bullet still lodged in his inner left thigh, a souvenir from the Spanish-American War.

Lawrence had belonged to the Negro Twenty-fourth Cavalry, a "buffalo soldier" so named by the Indians who feared the black soldiers, convinced that their black, "woolly" hair and beards were evidence that they were mystical beings: half men, half buffalo. He had come to Utah when the Twenty-fourth was transferred to Fort Douglas, cradled on the east bench of the Salt Lake Valley, and remained behind when, four years later, the cavalry was restationed in the Philippines.

Lawrence's entry into clock repair was happenstance. He had been the army's supply and requisition clerk, and, naturally gifted with his hands, had a knack for repairing rifles, wagons, and whatever the post required fixing. On one occasion, he repaired a pocket watch for one of the officers, who, in appreciation, made Lawrence a present of a manual on clock repair and nicknamed him "the horologist," a title Lawrence clung to, as it made him feel scientific.

Salt Lake City had few horologists, and as word spread of Lawrence's expertise, civilians began bringing him their timepieces as well.

When he left the cavalry, his clientele followed him

to his new shop. His clock-cleaning-and-repair business grew into a trading post of sorts, as people left notes of clocks they wanted to acquire or sell, and estate auctioneers found Lawrence to be a good wholesaler of their wares.

David met Lawrence through the purchase of a Black Forest cuckoo clock and instantly liked the man. There was a calmness in his motion, the temperament of one suited to repair the intricate. "Slow hands," David called it. But there was more. There was something comfortable in his manner that reminded David of earlier days. Growing up in the womb of the Eureka mine, David had worked and lived with black men, listened to their stories of injustices and enjoyed their company. In the depth of a mine, all men were black, and he had learned to appreciate people for their souls. The two men spent hours talking about clocks, California, and the cavalry.

Though both were fascinated by clocks, they were so for vastly different reasons. Where David saw immortality in the perpetual motion of the clocks' function, Lawrence was fascinated by the mechanism itself, and for hours on end, he would lose himself in a brass clockwork society—a perfect miniature world where all parts moved according to function. And every member had a place.

◆

As the falling sun stretched the remnant shadows of the day, David rapped on the door of Lawrence's shack.

"Lawrence?"

A soft, husky voice beckoned him in.

David stepped inside. Lawrence sat on a cot in the corner of the darkened room, a single candle cast flickering slivers of light across the man's face. In his hand was a smoldering pipe, which glowed orange-red.

"Sit down," he said. "Sit down."

The dwelling consisted of one room divided by function: the living quarters toward the east and the shop toward the west, separated by a plethora of clocks and a heavy table covered with clockwork, candles, and dripped wax.

Lawrence was proud of his humble furnishings: a small, round-topped table, splintered and worn in parts with odd-lengthed legs to hold it steady on the shack's unlevel floor. Around the table were three chairs, each of different manufacture. His bed was a feather mattress set on a home-built wooden frame and covered with the thick wool army blankets and roll he had slept on for nearly forty years. In the corner of the room, a potbelly stove sat on a stone-and-concrete platform. Where the room wasn't illuminated by the stove, it was lit by kerosene army lamps that hung from the rafters.

There were no windows, though they would have been unusable, as Lawrence had stacked firewood across the outside wall of his home.

David sat down on one of the chairs near the round table. "I brought the money for the pocket watch." He laid a wad of bills on the table.

"Thank you."

"Who was that woman I passed on the way around?"

"Big woman? Tha's Miss Thurston. The preacher's wife."

"What did she want?"

"Same thing she always wants."

"Which is?"

"Wantin' to get me out to the colored church." Lawrence shook his head in wonder. "Woman gets talkin' and soon ain't talkin' to me no more, but like she preachin' to a congregation. Gets herself all riled up about sinners and heathens and their sorry souls. I think it must make her feel good. Like she talked some sense into me."

"Did she?"

Lawrence frowned. "Don't rightly know what to reckon of it all. S'pose there is a heaven, I wanna know what kinda heaven it be. Is it a heaven for white folks? Or is it a different heaven for colored folk and white folk? What you make of it?"

David shrugged. "I am not an expert. I have only been to church on a few occasions. It seems to me that people who spend their lives dreaming about the gold-paved streets and heavenly mansions of the next life are no different than those who waste their time dreaming about it in this life. Only with a poorer sense of timing."

Lawrence responded in low, rumbling laughter reserved for when he found something particularly amusing. He clenched down on his pipe. "Never thought of it that way," he replied.

"The way I see it, it's not about what you are going to get, it's about what you become. Divinity is doing what is right because your heart says it's right. And if that puts you on the wrong side of the pearly gates, seems you would be better off on the outside."

Lawrence took in a long draw on his pipe. "You could've been a philos'pher."

Just then, in the dancing radiance of the candles, David noticed something he had never seen before, despite his many visits. Across the room, amidst the squalor of metal springs, and the shells and corpses of clocks, was what appeared to be a shrouded sculpture slightly protruding from beneath a cloth sheet.

"What is that in the corner? Under the cloth?"

Lawrence lowered his pipe. "Tha's my angel. Jus' this mornin' had some help and we brought her up from the cellar."

"Angel?" David walked over to the piece.

"Real Italian marble," Lawrence said.

David pulled a floor clock back from the sculpture and lifted the drape, exposing a stone sculpture of a dove-winged angel. Its seraphic face turned upward and its arms were outstretched, raised as a child waiting to be lifted. David ran his fingers over its smooth surface.

"This is a very expensive piece. Probably worth a hundred dollars or more. Is it new?"

"Had it for nearly six years, jus' never take her out of the cellar."

David admired the sculpture. "How did you come by this?"

"Right after I left the cavalry, I did some work for a minister. Fixed his church's steeple clock. Took me 'bout the whole summer. Problem is, before I got done, the church treasurer run off with all their buildin' money. So the minister asks me if I won' take this angel for payment."

David stepped away from the statue, rubbing his hand along its surface once more.

"Why didn't you sell it?"

Lawrence shook his head. "Don't need nuthin'." "Nuthin' you can buy." He tapped his pipe against the table, looking suddenly thoughtful. "Way I figgur, black man got no r'spect in this life. So I was thinkin' when I die, they put this angel here on my grave. Somebody walks by, even white folks, see that fine angel. 'Looks like real Italian marble,' they say. 'Mighty fine. Mus' be someone real important has that kinda monument. Mus' be a rich man or a military officer,' and they go on like that." Lawrence's eyes reflected red from the smoldering pipe, but seemed to glow beneath their own power. "Black man don' get much r'spect in this life."

David looked at Lawrence and nodded slowly as the night's silence filled the humble shack.

CHAPTER FIVE

The Presumption

" MaryAnne came into the office today. I was surprised to see her, as it was her Sabbath. I was much too forward and I fear I have frightened her. I am clumsy with romance."

DAVID PARKIN'S DIARY. MAY 13, 1908

avid disliked suits and never wore them on Sunday when he came in to the office to work alone. He was intent over a stack of papers on his desk when MaryAnne's presence startled him.

"Miss Chandler. What brings you here?"

"I did not finish my letters."

David stood. "Monday is soon enough."

"I did not want to fall behind. You have been so very busy."

David smiled, pleased for her concern.

"I think I would be worried if you could keep up." He

walked over to her. "Thank you, Miss Chandler, but go on home and rest. We have a full week ahead."

She put her hands in her coat pockets.

"Yes, sir."

Just then, a Westminster chime denoted a quarter of one. Both looked at the clock.

"I have not had supper, Miss Chandler. Would you care to join me? Perhaps at the Alta Club?"

MaryAnne smiled. "Thank you, Mr. Parkin, but if I am not needed, I should be off to church."

David nodded. "Yes. Of course. I suppose that I should go on home as well. Catherine is expecting me."

MaryAnne looked at him as if she had just been informed of some terrible news. She knew of no women in David's life. She tried to dismiss the thought and turned to leave, then paused at the doorway.

"May I ask you something, Mr. Parkin?"

"Of course."

"Who is Catherine?"

"Catherine is my housekeeper."

MaryAnne appeared relieved and turned to go, but David stopped her.

"Any other inquiries, Miss Chandler?"

She smiled playfully. "Now that you ask, I have wondered what makes a man collect clocks? And so many of them at that."

David studied her face, then leaned forward as if to reveal some great secret.

"It is because I need more time."

MaryAnne met his eyes and, for the first time in David's presence, laughed. It was a beautiful, warm laugh and David found it nourishing and laughed in turn.

"You have a wonderful laugh, Miss Chandler."

"Thank you."

"The truth is, I have wondered the same." He walked over to a cuckoo clock and lifted a brass pine-cone-shaped weight. "I am sure there are those who think me mad. As a boy, I had a penchant for collecting things. When I turned twenty-one, I received the first clock of my collection. It was my father's pocket watch." He suddenly stopped. "May I get you some tea? Peppermint?"

"Yes. Thank you." She started to rise. "I shall get it."

"Miss Chandler, please, sit down. I can manage." He brought the tea service over to his desk, poured two cups of tea, handed one to MaryAnne, then sat down on the arm of a nearby chair.

"I only drink peppermint tea. It's the one habit I borrowed from the English."

"Peppermint tea is an American concoction."

"Oh. Then I must just like it."

MaryAnne laughed again.

"I lived in Santa Rosa, California, at the time—when I turned twenty-one," he clarified. "It was the year my father died. It was also the same year that I first donned a pair of eyeglasses and acknowledged the creeping vines of age that entwine our lives."

MaryAnne nodded.

David looked back at a row of clocks. "I have wondered if I am deluding myself with these, that I am buying time—surrounding myself with man-made implements of immortality." He looked back at MaryAnne. "Whatever the reason, my fascination has grown into a full-blown obsession. My home is besieged with them."

"I would like to see—" MaryAnne stopped herself midsentence at the realization that she had just invited herself to a man's home.

"I would like to show you," David answered. He sat back in his chair and slowly sipped his tea. "I am curious, Miss Chandler. Do you like it here?"

"Here?"

"At my company."

"Very much, I think. More so than my other employment."

"You do not seem to socialize much with the other secretaries on the floor."

"You do not employ me to socialize."

David smiled. "The proper answer," he replied. "You work hard for nobility."

MaryAnne gazed at him. "Are you teasing me?"

He quickly set down his cup, anxious that he might have offended her again. "No. Not at all."

She took a sip of tea to hide her smile, then cradled the cup in her hands.

"I have always had to work hard, Mr. Parkin. My father left England because he had been disinherited for marrying my mother—a common woman of whom my grandparents disapproved. We had little when we arrived in America and less when my father passed away. As soon as I was able, I had to assist in my family's support. My mother passed on two years ago. So I am alone now."

"Have you any siblings?"

"I have a brother. But he returned to England more than six years ago. He sent money for a while—when times were better."

David quietly digested the information, then rested his chin on the back of his clasped hands. "May I ask you something of a personal nature?"

She hesitated. ". . . Yes."

"Are there men in your life?"

"Men?"

"Suitors."

She hesitated again, embarrassed. "There are a few I cannot seem to discourage."

"That is your goal? With men?"

"With these men. I know them too well to marry them, Mr. Parkin."

David nodded, then set down his tea. "Miss Chandler, I would prefer that you not call me Mr. Parkin."

"What would you have me call you?"

"David. Please call me David."

She considered the request. "I do not think I would feel comfortable in front of my coworkers."

David sighed. "I would not want you to feel uncomfortable, Miss Parkin."

"Miss Parkin?"

His face turned bright crimson as he suddenly realized his slip. "Miss Chandler," he stammered.

Suddenly the amusement faded from MaryAnne's eyes. She turned from him and stood.

"I must go."

"Must you?"

"It would be best."

There was an uncomfortable lull.

"I am sorry, MaryAnne. Perhaps I seem like your last supervisor who wanted you to sit on his lap."

"No, I did not mean . . ."

"My intentions are honorable. I would never seek to take advantage. . . . It is just . . ."

MaryAnne stared at him with anticipation. He turned away from her gaze.

"I have never met anyone quite like you. I am nearly thirty-four and have no real lady friends. Not that there are not interested females. Unfortunately, there are too many." He frowned. "They are attracted to money and status and cannot see my faults for my wealth. Though I have no doubt that marriage would open their eyes." His voice softened. "I feel very comfortable in your presence."

MaryAnne glanced briefly into his eyes, but said nothing.

"I am very sorry, Miss Chandler, I have made you uncomfortable. Forgive me. I shall not broach the subject again."

MaryAnne looked down. "Mr. Parkin, there are just things that—" She stopped herself midphrase. "I think that I must go now."

She slowly walked over to the doorway, followed by David's sad stare. She stopped and looked back at him.

"Good day, Mr. Parkin."

"Good day, Miss Chandler."

◆

Catherine pushed the drawing room door open with her shoulder and entered carrying a silver tray with a sterling tea service. The drapes were drawn tight and David sat on a haircloth love seat, staring into the crackling fire that provided the room's only illumination.

For Catherine bringing tea to the drawing room was a familiar ritual, established years before David had purchased the house; in a sense, Catherine had come with the house. Her former employer, the mansion's previous owner, fleeing the cold Salt Lake City winters for the refuge of the southern Utah sun, had left behind

Catherine, his young housemaid, and Mark, his footman, to consummate the sale of the property, then seek employment elsewhere. When David arrived, he found the house larger than he imagined and emptier than he expected. As he was now alone, he entreated the two to remain. They gladly accepted and quickly became part of his family. The first year, David had tried to persuade Catherine to call him by his first name, without success, and he eventually abandoned the undertaking.

"Excuse me, Mr. Parkin, I brought some tea."

David turned, his trance seemingly broken. "Oh. Thank you."

She left the service on a bird's-eye-maple parlor table next to his chair.

"Mr. Flake brought the French clock. I had him leave it in the parlor." She turned to leave, then stopped. "Are you well, sir?"

He sighed. "I am well enough, I suppose. Thank you for asking."

She turned again to leave.

"Catherine."

"Yes, sir."

"May I ask you something?"

"Certainly."

"As a woman . . . you being a woman . . ."

Catherine looked at him blankly.

"I meant . . . Oh, I sound foolish. How shall I ask this?" He appeared flustered with his inability to communicate his question. "What kind of man am I?"

Catherine looked confused. "I do not know how to answer that."

"I mean . . . do women, would a woman, find me attractive?"

"You are very handsome."

"I do not mean quite that. I mean . . . am I the kind of man a woman would want to marry? Or am I too long alone? Am I too rough? Do I say the wrong things?" His brow furled. "I need not ask that." David looked down. "I suppose it is no secret that I am fond of MaryAnne. Everyone seems to know it but her. Or perhaps she does not wish to know. Have you met MaryAnne?"

Catherine tilted her head thoughtfully. "I have only seen her from a distance, though Mark tells me she is very pleasant."

"Yes. She is very pleasant. She always says the right thing—has the proper answer." He took a sip of tea. "A skill I obviously lack."

Catherine smiled kindly. "Mr. Parkin, you are a very

good and kind man. Any woman would be fortunate to have you."

David looked up. "Thank you, Catherine."

"Good night, sir."

"Good night, Catherine."

She stopped at the threshold. "I spoke forthright, sir. Any woman would consider herself fortunate."

"Thank you," he repeated softly, then turned back toward the fire and lost himself in his thoughts.

◆

In the next nine weeks, as spring gave way to the oppression of summer, David noticed peculiarities in MaryAnne's behavior. It seemed to him that she was unusually preoccupied, and even her motion had taken on a peculiar deliberateness. At first, he had blamed himself for the change, attributing it to his "presumptuous blunder," until the peculiarities began to manifest themselves in more physical ways.

One afternoon, David heard her slowly climbing the stairway. She was winded when she reached the top of the stairs, and caught the railing, breathing heavily. Her face was flushed and she brushed her forehead with the back of her hand. David had watched her curiously from his doorway. When she saw him, she dropped her hand back to her side and walked quickly past him. David followed her. She sat down at her desk and began to type, ignoring his presence so deliberately as to acknowledge it.

David interrupted her. "Miss Chandler, are you well? You look peaked."

"I am fine," she replied. She did not look up, obviously avoiding his eyes. David continued to stare at her. "I'm concerned. You have not seemed yourself of late."

"Are you unsatisfied with my work?"

"No," he said firmly. "My concern is personal."

MaryAnne just bowed her head. Then, unexpectedly, she raised a hand to wipe a tear from her cheek.

The silence lengthened into an uncomfortable lull. David turned to leave.

MaryAnne took a deep breath. "David, may we speak?"

He stopped. It was the first time she had called him by his name and he knew that this was a matter of great significance.

"Of course. In my office."

Inside, he offered her a chair, then, after shutting the

door, returned to his desk and leaned against its front edge.

She looked down, catching tears in a handkerchief, then swallowed and looked up into his face.

"There is a reason I have behaved so peculiarly." She paused to gain courage. "David, I am with child."

The words had a strange effect on him. He sat back on the desk, as if his legs would fail him, and slowly shook his head. "I am such a fool. I did not know you were married."

She lowered her head in shame. "I'm not. Nor will I be." She wiped her cheeks, then cradled her face in her hands. "I am so sorry. I should have told you sooner, but . . ." She stopped, unable to continue.

"Yes?" he gently coaxed.

She took a breath. "Shortly before I came to work with you I was betrothed to be married. I was so foolish. He had pledged to me his love and I did not want to displease him. We were to be married this April." She looked up. "When he found out I was with child, he beat me."

The room was quiet except for the sound of the clocks.

"Why didn't you tell me before?"

"I was afraid."

"For your employment?"

She nodded, wiping away more tears. "I am all alone; I need the wages to care for my child. At first, I was afraid that you would not hire me if you knew. After I came to know you, I realized that it would not matter—that you would have hired me anyway. But by then I . . ."

David leaned forward.

". . . I was . . . Oh, this must sound so strange!"

"No," he said gently. "Go on, MaryAnne."

She looked away from him, then buried her head in her hands.

"I was beginning to have other feelings for you. I was afraid you would disapprove of me." She began to cry harder. The sound of the clocks seemed to increase in volume, interrupted by MaryAnne's occasional sobbing. Suddenly, David stepped forward and crouched down next to her chair. "There is a solution," he said gently.

MaryAnne lowered the handkerchief from her eyes.

"You could marry me."

She looked at him in disbelief, then covered her eyes with the handkerchief again. "Oh, David. Please do not play with me."

"No, I wouldn't."

She looked back up into his eyes. "You offer me yourself?"

"If it proves a bad bargain . . ."

"David? You would marry me with another man's child?"

David nodded, trying to coax a smile from her tear-streaked face.

For a moment, her eyes flashed brightly with hope, then extinguished almost as quickly. "It would be wrong for you, David. How could you?"

David took her hand in his. It was the first time that he had touched her in this way and it filled him with a strange electricity.

"In the wedding vow, they say for better or for worse. In sickness and in health. For richer or poorer. It would seem that the only thing certain about the alliance is a lot of uncertainty."

MaryAnne looked into his eyes. His gaze was direct and kind.

"I am not afraid of uncertainty or responsibility—it is what life is made of. But I am afraid that I will not meet another woman like you. And that you will not have me." The room fell silent except for the ticking of the clocks.

"David. I would be honored to be your wife."

David's eyes moistened. "I love you, MaryAnne." The words had come spontaneously, and he realized as he spoke them that it was the first time in his adult life that he had used the phrase. MaryAnne sensed the earnestness of his words and more tears welled up in her already moist eyes, then, before she could say anything, David pressed his lips against hers and gently kissed her.

MaryAnne pulled back suddenly and smiled. "I have a confession, David. Do you recall that Sunday when you accidentally called me Miss Parkin?"

David grinned, still embarrassed by the slip.

"Yes."

"It pleased me. I felt foolish, like a schoolgirl, but I called myself MaryAnne Parkin all afternoon. I liked the sound of my name with yours."

"MaryAnne Parkin," David repeated. His face stretched into a broad smile. "Yes," he said, nodding his head. "There is something very natural about the confederacy of our names. . . . Perhaps it was meant to be."

CHAPTER SIX

The Engagement

"A conspiracy of florists, caterers, and clergy have done too well a job of shrouding the virtues of the elopement."

DAVID PARKIN'S DIARY. JULY 5, 1908

he many surreys and fewer motor coaches began arriving at the Parkin mansion at seven, dispensing their affluent cargo at the doorstep, then pulling off into the field alongside the house. The sudden engagement announcement had caused no small stir among the local society, and the party was considered an affair not to be missed.

Inside, David, dressed in black tails with a white, fish-scale vest and band tie, stood in the drawing room surrounded by a group of businessmen from the Alta Club, while Catherine scurried back and forth managing a bevy of servants and seeing to the details of the affair.

Meanwhile, Victoria Marie Piper, a woman of considerable social and physical presence, had taken it upon herself to find the bride-to-be and discovered MaryAnne in the parlor in the east wing, where she had been waiting for David. Victoria swept into the room in a high-necked peach gown, encircled by a pink feather boa. At first glance, the dress might have been mistaken for a wide-hooped crinoline, as it broadened out enough to obstruct the corridor. In reality, it was only the woman.

Crossing the room with a small plate piled with cake in one hand and a china tea cup in the other, she marched up to MaryAnne and formally introduced herself.

"Miss Chandler, I am Victoria Marie Piper, of the Boston Pipers," she prated. "I am embarrassed to admit that we have not yet been introduced at any of the functions. Are you new to the city?"

MaryAnne blushed. "No. I have just not been to any . . . functions."

"Oh," she said abruptly. "Then how were you introduced to David?"

MaryAnne smiled innocently. "I was David's secretary."

The woman made no attempt to conceal her horror. "Oh," she gasped. "An office girl." She took a step back. "There are such dreadful stories about the office, but I am sure they do not apply to you," she said, looking down at MaryAnne's slightly protruding stomach. "Myself, I do not think it a woman's place, but what do I know of such things? I am too old-fashioned and probably too sensible for my own good," she said, flourishing a corpulent hand in dramatic gesture.

MaryAnne glanced towards the door, hoping that David would soon appear and rescue her. The woman took another bite of cake, then chased it down with tea. "Do you know David well?" she pried.

"I met him last spring," MaryAnne answered. "I have not known him for very long."

Victoria's face contorted in pretense to some awful knowledge. "Well, I would be ill used to not warn you of David. He is a controversial sort."

"Controversial?"

"It is quite well known." She set her plate on the linen cloth of a buffet, then leaned close to MaryAnne. "He associates quite openly with the Negroes and makes absolutely no attempt to hide it. It is as if he is not ashamed of it."

MaryAnne felt her cheeks flush with indignation. Victoria continued.

"You should be apprised. Of course, I should be pleased if this was the worst of his vices. There is much more that you should know." She paused to fan herself. "But this is not the time or place. It is disloyal of me to eat his cake and poison his name."

"Yes," MaryAnne replied, "perhaps you should just poison his cake and be done with it."

The woman glared at MaryAnne. Just then, David entered the room. Victoria's mouth pursed in a garish smile. "Oh, David, how are you?"

"The state of my health cannot possibly be of any concern to you, Victoria. What gossip are you boring MaryAnne with?"

"Oh, David, you have such an imagination," she drawled, turning to MaryAnne. "We really must have tea sometime, dear. Before the wedding." Her words lifted in a cruel crescendo. "I have so much to tell you." She took her plate and strutted out of the room. MaryAnne breathed a sigh of relief.

David grinned. "So you met Victoria."

"I am afraid I have offended her."

"It speaks well of you to offend Victoria."

MaryAnne stifled a laugh.

"Though one should not be too hard on the woman. She cannot help but turn up her nose."

"And why is that?"

He pointed to his throat. "Her double chin."

"David, you are awful."

"Yes, but I am honest. Are you bored?"

"I feel a bit out of place."

"As do I. This affair reeks of pretension. It is like lard frosting without the cake. Of course, the truly criminal thing is that it is our affair!"

MaryAnne laughed heartily. "Oh, David, you make me happy." She sighed. "It is so good to laugh."

"I drink your laughter, MaryAnne. It intoxicates me." David took her hand and led her out onto the back patio overlooking the garden walkway. The July air was cool and the waning sickle of a moon dimly lit the cobblestone walkway below.

"So what did Victoria have to say?"

"Nothing worth repeating, I'm afraid."

"You should know that I love gossip about myself."

"Then I will tell you. She says that you are controversial and associate with the Negroes."

"If Victoria is nothing, she is honest. Have I lost you now?"

"She has endeared you to me. You should have seen her face when she learned I was your secretary. She kept looking down at my stomach."

"I would be disappointed in her if she had not noticed."

"Why does she act so?"

"Because Victoria is the worst kind of society. She is not old money or new money, but somewhere in between, so she is forever trying to prove that she belongs somewhere in society. You, my love, simply are not of their caste. Of course, neither am I, but as I am richer than they, and as money is their God, or at least their idol, they must bow. But they despise doing it." David smiled indulgently. "Money, as they say, is always chic."

MaryAnne suddenly looked down and leaned back against the railing. "David, how will marrying me affect your social standing?"

David laughed. "Very well, I think, now that I have

someone I care to socialize with." He paused, studying her sad countenance. "MaryAnne, you are thinking of your mother and father. It is similar in a way, is it not?"

MaryAnne nodded.

"Except our story has a happy ending. Besides, I believe the 'Victorias' of my world are happy for my decision. I am certain they believe a woman, if not able to civilize me, will at least round off the rough edges."

MaryAnne kissed his cheek. "How goes it downstairs?"

"Awful. When the mayor entered, he handed Lawrence his coat."

"Oh, my. What did you do?"

"I had just entered the foyer, so I greeted Lawrence as a war hero, flattered the coat he held, and asked if I could hang it for him."

"Oh, my," she repeated. "What did the mayor do?"

"He was florid. My only regret is that Victoria was not present. A good fainting is guaranteed to get a party into the social column."

MaryAnne laughed again.

"How was your first day off work?" David asked.

"I missed you." She sighed. ". . . But not Gibbs."

David smiled. "You know, he is to be my best man."

"As long as I get you at the end of the day, I do not much care." MaryAnne clasped her hands on her stomach and smiled dreamily. "Catherine and I found the most elegant wedding dress. It was quite expensive."

"Shall I sell the business?"

"Do not tease me. I feel awkward spending your money. It is improper of me to even speak of it."

"MaryAnne, it is wonderful having someone I care to spend it on. As your husband, I insist that you always allow me the luxury of spoiling you."

MaryAnne draped her arms around her fiancé. "What makes you think that I do not already have everything?"

"The proper answer," he replied. "Always the proper answer."

◆

"If the heavens were to open and a host of Angels descend, they could not have produced such an effect on my soul as MaryAnne descending the chapel staircase for our wedding."

DAVID PARKIN'S DIARY. AUGUST 11, 1908

It was common knowledge, if anything among the city's social elite was to be deemed common, that

David Parkin was not one for ostentatious display. So the extravagance of the wedding was a surprise to all, and even the most jaded admitted to being suitably impressed.

The preparation for the wedding had taken five weeks of daily attention from the time of the engagement announcement to the nuptial day, and Catherine, as instructed by David, saw to it all, conducting a symphony of florists, servants, and caterers. At one point, a florist wryly remarked, "Madam, I was told this was to be a wedding, not a coronation."

"This wedding will want for nothing," Catherine retorted. "Mr. Parkin expects an affair unlike one this city has ever witnessed. And nothing less."

The florist prudently apologized.

In the days leading up to the event, David considered MaryAnne's bridal gift with great care. Jewelry was customary, so in addition to the wedding ring, he had purchased a large diamond pendant, which, in afterthought, he found unsatisfying, as he thought gems generally cold, and the bauble's beauty easily outdone by MaryAnne's. Only two days before the wedding, the second gift arrived from a New York City brokerage and was promptly sequestered in the upstairs parlor behind a locked door. David was pleased by this gift most of all, and looked forward to its giving.

The morning of the wedding, Gibbs arrived early at the house to take David for breakfast. The florist and his assistants, under Catherine's watchful eye, were already busy wiring flowers to the chandeliers, railings, and brass hardware as David greeted Gibbs at the door. David was dressed in a high-necked, white linen shirt with a twelve-button silk vest. His tailcoat was pin-striped and cut at the waist. He wore charcoal trousers and a black silk top hat.

"Gibbs! Nice to see you, old man."

Gibbs embraced him in the open doorway. "He was warned against the woman, She was warned against the man, And if that won't make a weddin', why there's nothin' else that can!'"

"So there you have it, you are responsible for this affair."

"I do not take responsibility."

"It would be a good thing for you to do."

Gibbs smiled. "I am happy for you, David."

"I am happier for myself."

"I confess more than once I have been reminded of scripture about coveting a man's wife."

"You still have a few hours before it will be sin. Have you the license?"

Gibbs pulled the elaborate scrolled parchment from the breast pocket of his coat.

"Then you are an accomplice. And the ring?"

Gibbs nodded. "What a ring, David!" he exclaimed as he lifted the small box from his pocket. "Has Mary-Anne seen it?"

David shook his head. "Not yet. It is one of the day's surprises."

Gibbs replaced the box and took two cigars from the breast pocket of his coat and offered one to David, as he turned looking out to his motorcar. "Well, David, we best be off. Your single carefree moments are fleeting." He grinned sardonically. "And with a new wife, perhaps your fortune as well."

◆

At the dictate of English custom, the wedding was scheduled for twelve noon. Ten minutes before the hour, David, with Gibbs by his side, entered the chapel and proceeded directly to the altar.

As the last noon strike of the steeple's clock resonated in a metallic echo, the church organ erupted in brilliant sforzando. MaryAnne appeared at the top of the circular staircase, and the entire congregation rose to their feet as much in collective awe as ceremony. She was radiant in a hand-embroidered ivory dress that laced down the front, corseting her narrow, though expanding, hourglass figure. Delicate lace gloves rose past her elbows and a cathedral-length veil cascaded down her back, held in place by a simple orchid wreath.

David could not take his eyes off his bride as she descended the stair, flanked by Catherine and preceded by Catherine's five-year-old niece, who dropped white rose petals before them as they passed beneath the great floral arches of white peonies and apple blossoms.

For the first time in his life, David truly felt fortunate. When MaryAnne reached the altar, he leaned close.

"You look stunning, my bride."

MaryAnne blushed as they knelt together before the clergyman on a silk pillow facing an altar of white-and-gold–leafed alderwood.

The organ ceased and MaryAnne handed the robed priest a prayer book. He thanked her, opened the book, and cleared his throat.

"Who giveth this woman to be married to this man?"

There was a sudden and uncomfortable silence. It had been discussed previously that there was no one to give MaryAnne away. It was an error, born of habit, on the clergyman's part, and he instantly recognized his blunder.

MaryAnne looked up. "God does, Your Reverence."

The priest smiled as much at her cleverness as her sincerity.

"So he does, my dear."

He looked out over the congregation. "Dearly beloved, we are gathered here today to unite this couple in holy matrimony according to God's holy ordinance. Are there any who object to the union of this couple?"

There was no response, though Victoria Piper took the opportunity to cough. The priest turned to the bride. "My dear, if you will repeat after me."

MaryAnne looked at David affectionately as she repeated the words of the vow until the priest said "till death do us part."

David looked into her face as a tear rolled down her cheek. "MaryAnne?" he asked gently. At her name, MaryAnne looked up at David. "Not until death, my love, but forever."

David smiled and his eyes moistened. "Forever," he repeated.

Catherine wiped a tear from her cheek.

The priest smiled and continued. "And thereto I give thee my troth."

MaryAnne took a deep breath. "And thereto I give thee my troth."

The priest then turned to David, who followed him in the oath with the proper and extemporaneous alterations. When they had completed their vows, the priest nodded to Gibbs, who handed David the ring. MaryAnne removed the glove from her left hand and handed it to Catherine, who took it, and delicately folded it in half, then took MaryAnne's engagement ring and bouquet. MaryAnne offered David her hand.

David held out the ring. It was an exquisite diamond marquise of extraordinary cut and color, framed with sapphires, and set in a woven, white-gold band.

MaryAnne was breathless. "David!"

He smiled at her joy as he slid the ring onto her finger.

The priest bestowed a final blessing on the couple and the organ roared to life. David stood first, and offering his bride his right hand, helped her to her feet.

She took his arm and, after Catherine had turned MaryAnne's train, they departed down the aisle. David shook a river of hands as they hurried out of the church to a flower-strewn carriage where a formally attired coachman sat waiting. At the couple's approach, the driver laid a step down and helped MaryAnne and then David into the carriage. He encouraged the horses with a flick of his whip and the carriage lurched forward.

When they were a distance from the church, David kissed his bride, then leaned back contentedly. "I would like to give you one of your wedding gifts now."

MaryAnne smiled. "One of?"

"Remember, my love, now that you are mine, it is my prerogative to spoil you." He handed her a small box wrapped in elegant white tissue. She tore back the paper, then lifted the lid. Inside lay the teardrop diamond pendant. It shone with exquisite brilliance, reflecting the afternoon sun.

"Oh, David," MaryAnne said softly. "You have made me a queen."

"No, MaryAnne. I have merely provided the proper accoutrements."

He raised the pendant, reached around her neck,

and clasped its golden rope. It encircled her neck beautifully, falling just above her cleavage. She laid her head against his shoulder and looked down at her wedding ring. "I promise you that I will be a good wife."

"And, my love, I promise to be a good husband and friend. Your other present is back at our home."

"Our home," she repeated softly.

◆

The wedding-brunch arrangements had been made for the garden, and it had never seen such splendor. No expense was spared. Long-shafted oil lamps with ribbons and orange blossoms tied around their supports decorated the grounds. Peacocks strutted about the yard in full plume between the white-laced tables that dotted the estate. The wedding cake itself was an elegant feat of architecture, six-tiered and bedecked with freshly cut white and peach roses.

The food was served from the high-pitched, flower-laced gazebo. The menu had been especially selected and was abundant with cakes and bonbons, raw and fricasseed oysters, bouillon, cobblers, ices and coffee and entrées of crab, lobster, quail, and Cornish hens.

When the brunch had concluded, the caterers began the task of boxing and wrapping the wedding cake for the guests, and the couple moved inside to the elaborate drawing room, where white roses covered and concealed the room's chandeliers. Lilies and pink roses adorned the fireplace mantel and flowered vines encircled the mahogany pillars. David and MaryAnne stood before a backdrop of palms to meet their guests.

When the room's clocks struck five, David turned to his bride. "I would like to give you your wedding present now." Taking leave of their guests, he took her hand and led her upstairs to the parlor, where he removed a thin key from his vest and unlocked the door.

At his request, she closed her eyes, and taking his hand, followed him into the room.

"You may open your eyes."

MaryAnne opened her eyes. Before her stood a majestic grandfather's clock, larger and more magnificent than anything David had previously collected. It stood nearly eight feet in height, and the casing was ornately carved in floral renderings. Detailed pillars flanked the clock's hood, which rose in two swan-necked pieces of carved mahogany facing inward toward a central finial spire. The white-faced dial was hand-painted and bordered by ornately patterned brass spandrels, preserved beneath a lead-crystal door that locked with a skeleton key.

"David, it is the most beautiful clock."

David studied her face anxiously. "Do you like it?"

She stepped forward to her gift and ran her fingers across its exquisite carvings. "It is so ornate. Yes. Very much."

David joined her. "I wanted the exterior to be as intricate as the interior clockwork. The chime is exquisite and unlike anything I have ever heard. It is angelic."

MaryAnne was enthralled. "I have never owned anything of such worth."

"May I tell you why I wanted to give you a clock?"

She turned to her groom. "There is greater significance than its beauty?"

David stared into the clock's face. "You once asked me why I collected clocks."

MaryAnne nodded.

"I have given this question a great deal of thought since then. A clock is a strange invention. A collection of cogs and gears that are always in motion, yet accomplish nothing. Not like a pump that provides water or a cotton gin that leaves something useful. A clock just moves without thought or meaning—worthless without interpretation." His eyes focused on the clock in condemnation. "It is just motion." He turned and looked into his new wife's eyes. "And so has been my life. I have moved, not with feeling, but because it is all that I could see to do. You have given my motion meaning."

MaryAnne looked into David's face. "I have given you my life, David."

"And in so doing, you have given me mine."

They embraced again, kissing at length. David smiled as they parted. "Let us be on our way!"

"Yes, my love."

◆

Gibbs was already outside with the hackney, loading the travel cases into the carriage. On the front step, MaryAnne hugged Catherine.

"Thank you, Catherine. You have made this day beautiful."

"I am so happy for you both. Take good care of him, MaryAnne. I love him dearly."

MaryAnne embraced her tighter. "How could you not, my sister."

After counting the cases, David took his bride by the hand and helped her up into the carriage.

Gibbs stood by the side of the carriage. "Good luck, David."

"Thank you, Gibbs. We will return in a fortnight. The company is in your hands."

CHAPTER SEVEN

Andrea

"I had never supposed the cost women bear in the perpetuation of the species. Nor that such courage could be had in such a petite frame."

DAVID PARKIN'S DIARY. JANUARY 17, 1909

MaryAnne's pains were still light when the hurry-up call went out to the midwife, one Eliza Huish. The woman was known as one of the most revered midwives in the city, and had given birth herself on eleven occasions.

Eliza arrived on horseback shortly before dusk. She was older than MaryAnne had expected; a stern, aged countenance worn into the matriarch's hard face. She was wide-hipped and buxom, her hair was streaked with gray and drawn back tightly in a bun with a few prodigal strands falling across her cheek. Her attire matched her manner. She was dressed austerely in a drab muslin dress partially concealed beneath a faded ivory apron, which carried the stains of previous deliveries. At her side was a worn carpetbag filled with the implements of her profession: herbs, ointments, tonics, and tattered rags.

"Waters not yet broke, Catherine?" she asked.

"No, ma'am."

The woman stopped at the room's threshold and surveyed the elaborate Victorian parlor, her eyes raised to the ornate frescoed ceiling. She was not likely to have seen such wealth before. The parlor was one of David's favorite rooms, and though he spent little time there, he endowed the room with his favorite collectibles, including MaryAnne's grandfather's clock. MaryAnne, at Catherine's suggestion, had chosen to birth in the parlor, as it was more convenient to the water closet and kept better temperature than the other upstairs rooms.

The woman sized up the room's occupants, then went to work with priggish fervor. Her first official act was to expel David from the room. In reluctant retreat, he left the parlor with his hands raised above his head and told Mark outside, "It is a time of female despotism."

"Why can't David be with me?" MaryAnne asked.

The question stunned the woman, who found the very wish unnatural and could see no reason why a woman should desire a man's presence at such an occasion.

"It is not a man's place when a woman is in travail," she said. "Only a woman can know what a woman is suffering."

MaryAnne was in no condition to argue and relinquished herself to the woman's government. The midwife placed a hand on MaryAnne's forehead, then walked to the foot of the bed and lifted MaryAnne's gown up to the waist, singing hymns beneath her breath as she worked. She poured virgin olive oil into her hands and began rubbing it into MaryAnne's hips and abdominal muscles.

"This'll stretch you out, darlin'. Make it a whole lot easier. Also brought along some Lydia Pinkham's vegetable compound. Fetch that from my satchel, Catherine. And the spoon."

Catherine lifted a brown glass bottle filled with the tonic. She leveled a spoonful and offered it to Mary-Anne, who made a face at the bitter substance.

"Two spoonfuls, Catherine. Works miracles with all

female ailments," the midwife said confidently, as she kneaded MaryAnne's thighs. After administering the dosage, Catherine pressed a cup of coffee to MaryAnne's lips, which she gratefully received. The woman wiped the oil from her hands onto a rag.

"How long since labor started?"

"She had the first strong pain shortly after noon. She started regular several hours ago," Catherine said. Her voice rose hopefully, then fell in disappointment. ". . . But they stopped just before you arrived."

MaryAnne sighed.

The women sat and looked at each other quietly.

"Would you care for something to eat, Eliza?" Catherine offered.

The woman nodded. "Thank you." She looked over at MaryAnne. "Haven't had a bite since breakfast."

Catherine excused herself, returning fifteen minutes later with a silver tray stacked with cut cucumbers, honey candy, pine nuts, and cream cheese and walnut sandwiches. The woman snacked on the fare, eventually joined by Catherine, who ate only to pass time. A half hour later, MaryAnne suddenly began breathing heavily. The midwife set down a sandwich and placed both hands on MaryAnne's stomach, concentrating on the contractions with professional intensity. Three minutes later, MaryAnne started into another. "There, that's a good start. Long pains, close together."

MaryAnne grimaced. "It's taking so long."

"It is natural, the first birth always takes longer. We'll likely be here all night." As if to emphasize her words, she glanced over her shoulder at the grandfather's clock. "There's a fine clock . . . help us time these pains."

A minute later, MaryAnne tensed again, then groaned with another contraction.

"Just breathe easy, darlin'. No sense making it any harder than it need be. First always takes longer," she repeated. "Seen a first labor once go up on two days . . . but once the water broke."

MaryAnne was oblivious to the chatter, concentrating on the strange forces that had seized her body.

In the next ten minutes, MaryAnne had gone through five more cycles.

"How do you feel now, darlin'?"

"I want to push," MaryAnne panted.

"Good, good. It's moving along right quickly now. You go right ahead and push with the next pain."

The woman wiped her forehead with her wide sleeves. Two minutes later, MaryAnne started into another contraction. As she began to push, her water broke. MaryAnne felt the sheet beneath her wet.

The midwife gasped. "Oh, dear." She stood looking at the bright red discharge. MaryAnne was bleeding heavily. The woman became suddenly grave. "Catherine, hurry now, get me some rags."

"What's wrong?" Catherine whispered.

"There may be separation of the afterbirth."

"What is wrong?" MaryAnne asked, her voice strained.

"A little bleeding, darlin'."

Catherine said nothing. MaryAnne was bleeding profusely.

MaryAnne looked up at the ceiling. "Is my baby all right?" She clenched for another contraction. Her voice pitched. "Catherine, where is David?"

"I don't know, MaryAnne."

"I want David," MaryAnne said between heavy breaths.

"It is not proper," the midwife returned, studying the continued flow of blood. MaryAnne sensed from the change in the woman's countenance that the crisis was greater than she confessed. Fifteen minutes passed beneath the clock's serpentine hands. The midwife's anxiety increased. MaryAnne began to feel light-headed.

"Is my baby still alive?"she asked again.

The woman did not answer. The blood continued to flow.

"Will I die?"

The midwife shook her head unconvincingly. "You will be well enough."

MaryAnne's breathing quickened with the onset of a new contraction. She did not believe the woman's reply. "Is there a chance that I will die?"

This time, the woman did not respond. MaryAnne exhaled, then clenched down with the pain. "If we are to die in travail it will be with David by my side."

The midwife looked up at Catherine. "Call the man."

At Catherine's summons, David quickly entered the dim room, his face bent in concern. He walked to the side of the bed and took MaryAnne's hand. It was impossibly cold. He glanced up at the midwife, who silenced him with a sharp shake of her head. His heart froze. She did not want to concern MaryAnne with the seriousness of her condition. How bad was it? He looked down at the foot of the bed and saw the pile of blood-soaked rags. He felt his stomach knot. MaryAnne was wet with perspiration. David held her hand as he blotted her forehead.

Oh, God, do not take her from me, he silently

prayed. I will give anything. He rubbed her hand to warm it. "You can do this, Mary. It will be all right. Everything will be all right."

"I am so cold."

David bit back his fear. "It will be all right, my love."

Just then, the midwife walked to the side of the bed and bent over MaryAnne. Her forehead was beaded in perspiration and her face bore a solemn, dark expression. There was no more time to shield MaryAnne from the truth of the crisis. "MaryAnne, the baby needs to come now." Her words came slowly, each weighted with emphasis. "You need to give birth now."

"I don't know how to!" she cried.

"You can do it, MaryAnne," she replied firmly. "Go ahead and push. The baby must come."

"Is my baby alive?"

The midwife said nothing. Catherine began to cry and turned away.

"Is my baby alive?!" she screamed.

"I don't know. It is the baby's sack which is bleeding, so the baby is in the gravest danger. But it is still your blood, and if it does not stop soon . . ."

A chill ran up David's spine. "Can't you just take the baby?!"

"No," MaryAnne said. David turned to her pensively. Her face was pallid and though her eyes were dim they did not veil her determination. "No, David."

David clasped her hand in both of his.

"Oh, MaryAnne."

"I don't want to leave you."

"You're not leaving me, MaryAnne. I won't let you leave me."

Eliza walked back down between MaryAnne's legs as she started into another contraction. Just then, a cuckoo clock erupted in festive announcement of the second hour, followed by a gay, German melody accompanying tiny, brightly colored figurines waltzing in small circles on a wooden track.

"I feel the baby!" Eliza was certain that she would first feel the afterbirth, nearly assuring the infant's demise. "MaryAnne, push again!"

"I feel as if all my insides are coming out."

"You are doing wonderfully."

"Yes, you are doing wonderfully." David was seeing a whole new side of his wife, and of life, and it filled him equally with awe and terror.

"Push again, darlin'."

MaryAnne closed her eyes tightly and pushed.

"I have its head!" she exclaimed. "The baby is alive!" MaryAnne cried out in pain and joy.

"One more push, Mary. Just one more."

MaryAnne obeyed and the child emerged, coated in blood and fluid. When she had taken the baby in her arms, the midwife looked up at David and MaryAnne, still breathing heavily. "You have a daughter." She severed and tied the umbilical cord, oiled off the baby, then laid her on MaryAnne's chest. MaryAnne took the infant in her arms and wept with joy. Eliza's stern, hazel eyes rested on David. "Now leave the room."

David beamed. "A daughter," he repeated. As he left the room, he paused at the threshold to smile at MaryAnne, who, with tears streaming down her cheeks, smiled back at him, proud of the tiny daughter she held.

◆

In the dark hallway outside the parlor, David sat alone on a padded fruitwood bench, a wall separated from the muffled cry of the newborn infant. His heart and mind still raced—much as one who, narrowly avoiding an accident, finds his heart pounding and his breath stolen.

On a walnut whatnot at the far end of the hall, an

antique French clock chimed delicately, denoting the half hour. He glanced down the hallway. His eyes were unable to discern the piece in the darkness. At one time, the clock had been the most valuable of his collection—an elaborate, gilded Louis XV mantel clock, signed by its long-dead creator. The clock's waist opened to expose a pendulum bob in the form of sun rays, and on its crown were two golden cherubs. In its base was set a musical box.

David had acquired the clock in the crowded Alfred H. King auction hall in Erie, Pennsylvania, a year after he had moved to Salt Lake City. He had paid nearly one thousand dollars more than he had intended to for the clock, the price escalating to match not its worth, but his desire. The day of the auction, he had visited the piece no fewer than a dozen times and obsessed over it, regarding all who came near it with wanton jealousy. He had never desired a piece so intensely and wanted the clock no matter the price.

That desire was a candle to the furnace he had just felt at MaryAnne's side. What he had prayed in desperation, he meant just as fervently in the peace of resolution—that he would truly have given everything he owned to know that MaryAnne would be all right.

◆

"We have chosen for our daughter the name of MaryAnne's mother—Andrea. What a thing it is to be introduced to one's child. I find a new side to my being that even the gentility of MaryAnne could not produce from my brutal soul."

DAVID PARKIN'S DIARY. JANUARY 18, 1909

The birth of the child was greeted with great celebration by the thirty-four employees at the Parkin Machinery Company. Knitted booties and gowns came in from all quarters, each secretary, or clerk's wife, attempting to outdo the other.

Lawrence brought Andrea a homemade rattle that he had crafted by bending brass strips into a ball and covering it with sewed leather, concealing inside two miniature harness bells.

Once again, the Parkin home was adorned with flowers, many from neighbors and business associates, but most from David, who felt as if he had completed a great bargain in marrying one lady and only five months later found himself with two.

If the child's sireship was David and MaryAnne's secret, it seemed of little importance, as the child could not have been more his. It gave David great pleasure to be told that the child looked like her father, and, curiously, Andrea seemed to resemble him more than his wife. This fact was so frequently called to attention that David finally asked MaryAnne if he bore a resemblance to Andrea's real father.

"You are her real father," she answered. When he pressed her harder, she only replied, "He was not so handsome."

Andrea was a pretty child with large, piercing brown eyes that rested above sculptured rose cheeks. At first, her hair came in platinum wisps that curled on top until it grew long and fell to her shoulders in gilded chestnut coils. She had the delicate features of a porcelain doll, and whenever MaryAnne took her out in public, they were accosted by other women who strained to catch a glimpse of the infant, then squealed in delight that such a petite creation should cross their path.

In a strange ritual not fully understood even by its practitioners, every acquaintance of the Parkins who possessed a male child staked their claim on Andrea for their son, which only served, if it were possible, to add to MaryAnne and David's pride.

◆

"*In the year* A.D. *69 the Roman emperor Vitellius paid the chief priest of Gaul, whose responsibility it was to determine the beginning and end of spring, a quarter of a billion dollars to extend spring by one minute. The emperor then boasted that he had purchased that which all man cannot. Time.*

"*Vitellius was a fool.*"

DAVID PARKIN'S DIARY. APRIL 18, 1909

With the birth of Andrea, David was born anew. If MaryAnne had given David's life meaning, Andrea gave meaning to his future. Since his own childhood had been spent in the blackness of mines and the company of adults, David had never been with children, and now he heralded each new stage of his daughter's development with the ecstasy of scientific discovery. The day Andrea first rolled over in her crib, he inwardly cursed the world that it had not stopped to acknowledge the marvel. It was as if he was finding the childhood he was denied, and, through Andrea, seized the wonder of it all—a child's world of stuffed dolls and menagerie animals sculpted in the clouds. The employees of the Parkin Machinery Company were informed on a daily basis of the baby's progress and were happily amused with this new side of their boss's personality. It was said at the office that David seemed happily distracted, though, in fact, he had just become more focused on the child, and, lest he miss her childhood, spent more time at home.

In late spring, necessity forced an extended business trip back East, which David returned home from a week early. Catherine met him at the door and took his coat and attaché case.

"Welcome home, sir."

"Thank you, Catherine. Where are MaryAnne and Andrea?"

"They are in the gazebo. May I take your shoulder bag?"

"Thank you, but no. These are gifts."

David passed through the house and out into the garden, where MaryAnne sat on the gazebo swing, gently rocking the baby she nursed at her breast. The yard was littered with the white popcorn blossoms of apricot trees, the crisp air filled with the perfume of the garden and the sounds of MaryAnne's hummed lullabies. MaryAnne, absorbed in a different world, looked up only when he was a few feet off.

"David!"

He smiled wide, laid down the heavy shoulder bag, kissed her, then, sitting down, pulled the blanket back, exposing the suckling child.

"What wonderful animals we are," he said. "It is so good to be home. You two have made my life very difficult. You have exposed me to the malady of homesickness."

"Then it is contagious," MaryAnne replied. "We have missed you so. How was the journey?"

"It is done." He leaned over and kissed Andrea on her head. "In my absence, I have thought a great deal about my business. I have decided that I miss my secretary."

"Yes?"

"I was hoping I could get her back."

"If you could accommodate two ladies for the position I may consider it."

He leaned back and breathed in the rich scent of lilac and apple blossom. "Spring breathes such life into this desert. I concluded the business faster than I, or they, planned."

"Was it productive?"

"Adequate." He suddenly smiled. "I have something to show you," he said excitedly. He released the straps of the shoulder bag, then extracted a gold-papered box from inside. He lifted the top of the box and parted the tissue. Inside lay a burgundy velvet dress with a black silk sash and white lace collar.

MaryAnne gasped. "It is beautiful!"

"I think we should try it on her," David suggested.

MaryAnne covered her mouth, then turned, trying to conceal her amusement.

"Why are you laughing?"he asked innocently.

"I am sorry." She chuckled. "David, it won't fit her for years!" With one hand, she lifted the dress out of the box.

He examined the garment then looked back down at the infant.

"Oh."

"It is a lovely dress. She will look beautiful in it." Her mouth lifted in a teasing smile. "When she is four or five." She laughed again.

"I am not much with sizes," he confessed. He reached again into his bag. This time, he lifted out a miniature wooden crate, then carefully extracted from its cotton boll packing a small porcelain music box, a carousel, hand-painted in pastel-and-gold adornment. He wound the instrument then held it out in the palm of his hand. It plucked a simple carnival tune as the carousel revolved and its intricate horses rose and fell in clockwork mechanism. At the sound of the music, Andrea turned from MaryAnne's breast to see the toy. She cood happily, reaching out to touch the tiny, prancing horses.

"It is wonderful! Where did you find such a toy?!"

"At a clock shop in Pennsylvania. The proprietor, a Mr. Warland, creates the most intriguing inventions."

"You give good gifts, David."

"I have a gift for you, too."

"What is it?"

"It's heavy. And it is rather different, but I thought you might like it." He reached into the sack, lifting out a wooden box of dark, burled walnut. Leather straps ran across the top over an intricately carved Nativity and fastened into silver buckles. On the opposite side were two brass hinges skillfully forged in the shape of holly leaves.

"It is beautiful. Is it to hold Christmas things?"

"It is not empty." David set the box next to Mary-Anne. She unfastened its silver clasps and drew back the leather straps, then opened the box slowly. The interior of the box was lined with wine-colored velvet and occupied by an ancient leather Bible, its cover delicate with age and adorned with gold-leafed engravings.

"Oh, David . . ."

"I thought you would like it. It is at least two hundred years old. I bought the Bible at an auction. Then I saw the box and thought it a good match."

"Sir."

David turned. He had not seen Catherine approach. She stood outside the gazebo, holding a calling card in her outstretched hand.

"Gibbs has left a message."

"Thank you."

David took the card. MaryAnne looked up from the box. "What is it?"

"Gibbs wishes to meet with me tomorrow. From the tone of the note, I suspect he is concerned about business matters."

"Is there something wrong?"

"Nothing." He lifted the carousel again, then, winding it, held it out for Andrea. "All is well."

◆

"In Philadelphia I had such fortune to discover a most unusual piece, a sixteenth-century brass-and-gold sundial that

duplicates the prophet Isaiah's biblical miracle of turning back time.

" 'Behold, I will bring again the shadow of the degrees, which is gone down in the sun dial of Ahaz, ten degrees backward. So the sun returned ten degrees, by which degrees it was gone down.'

ISAIAH 38:8

"The gilded sundial is lipped to hold water and on one edge a figurine, a Moor, holds taut a line which extends from the center of the dial. The sun's rays, when reflecting from the water, bends the shadow and, for two hours each day, turns back time. Its possessor was unwilling to part with it."

DAVID PARKIN'S DIARY. APRIL 17, 1909

The next day, at Gibbs' behest, David came early to work and attacked a pile of paperwork and financial documents. Not an hour into the day, there was a knock on the door. A grim-faced Gibbs pushed the door open.

"David, may we have a moment?"

"Certainly."

"How was Philadelphia?"

"I was only able to negotiate a partial price concession, but it is acceptable."

Gibbs frowned. In all the years he had known David, he rarely did not get what he wanted—and never dismissed compromise so readily.

"You look concerned, Gibbs. I received your card. What is troubling you?"

"I am concerned. Our sales are down considerably."

"Yes. I have seen the ledgers."

Gibbs sighed. "It is difficult without you here. You are still our best salesman. When we meet with the larger accounts, they are offended that you are not present. One asked me if they had fallen in our esteem."

David frowned. "Are we still making a profit?"

"We could be making more. There is such growth in this city."

David walked across the room and looked out the window to the traffic below. For a full minute he said nothing, then, in a softened voice, began to speak.

"When is it enough, Gibbs?"

"I do not know what you mean."

David raised his hands, his back still turned to his manager. "When are we profitable enough? When do I have enough money? I could not possibly spend all that I have in two lifetimes. Not in twenty lifetimes."

Gibbs leaned back in exasperation. "There has been

a great find of copper in the Oquirrh benches. There's talk of a large open pit mine to rival the world's largest. There are great opportunities. And we are missing them."

"You are right." David turned back around. "That is exactly what we are talking about. Lost opportunities. I can always make more money. But how shall I go about reclaiming a lost childhood? The only promise of childhood is that it will end." He paused in reflection. "And when it is gone, it is gone."

Gibbs sighed in frustration. "I am only trying to protect our interests."

"And I am not making it very easy for you to do your job." David walked over and put his hand on Gibbs's shoulder. "I appreciate you, and I will not let my business fail. Nor will I let you or any of my employees down. But right now I feel that I have finally found life. To leave it would be death. Do your best, Gibbs. But, for now, do it without me." His words trailed off in silence and Gibbs lowered his head in disappointment.

"Yes, David." He rose and walked from the room.

◆

"It would seem that my Andrea is growing so quickly, as if time were advancing at an unnatural pace. At times I wish it

were within my power to reach forth my hand and stop the
moment—but in this I err. To hold the note is to spoil the song."

DAVID PARKIN'S DIARY. OCTOBER 12, 1911

Two months before Andrea's third birthday, the cradle was taken up to the attic and an infant bed was brought in its place. The new bed was exciting to the small girl and represented freedom, which, to a child, is a poor requisite for sleep. David and MaryAnne found that it took more time to put her down each night.

One night, David finished reading a second story to Andrea, then, thinking himself successful in lulling her to sleep, leaned over and kissed her on the cheek.

"Good night," he whispered.

Andrea's eyes popped open. "Papa. You know what?"

David smiled in wonder at the child's persistence. "What?"

"The trees are my friends."

David grinned at the sudden observation. "Really?" He pulled the sheet up under her chin. "How do you know this?"

"They waved to me . . ."

David smiled.

". . . and I waved back."

David's smile broadened. He was astonished at the purity of the child's thought. "Andrea, do you know why I love you so much?"

"Yes," she replied.

"Why?" he asked, genuinely surprised that she had an explanation.

"Because I'm yours."

Strangely, Andrea's reply inflicted him with a sharp pang of dread. He forced a smile. "And you are right. Good night, little one."

"Good night, Papa," she replied sleepily and rolled over.

David did not return to his bedroom but retreated to the seclusion of the drawing room to think. After an hour, MaryAnne, dressed in her nightclothes, came for him. She quietly peered in. David sat in a richly brocaded green-and-gold chair. Several books lay next to him, though none was open. His head was bowed, resting in the palm of one hand. MaryAnne entered.

"David? Is business troubling you?"

He raised his head.

"No." His voice was laced with melancholy. "I have just been wondering."

MaryAnne came behind his chair and leaned over it, wrapping her arms around his neck.

"What have you been wondering, my love?"

"Shall we ever tell her?"

"Tell her?"

"That I am not her real father."

MaryAnne frowned. She came around and sat on the upholstered footstool before him. "You are her real father."

He shook his head. "No, I'm not. And I feel dishonest, as if I were hiding something from her."

"David, it isn't important."

"But shouldn't she be allowed the truth? I feel as if I am living a lie."

"Then it is the lesser of a much greater one."

"What is that?"

"Society's lie. The lie that claims that simply impregnating a woman makes a man a father." Her eyes glazed in loathsome recall. "The man who lay with me is not a father. He is not even a real man. I wonder that he is a member of our species."

David sat still, quietly weighing the intent of her words. "Have you seen him? Since our engagement?"

MaryAnne wondered why he had asked the question, but could not discern from his expression. "Once."

"You went to him?"

"David!" She took his hand. "That would be like emptying a cup of champagne to fill it with turned milk."

"You hate him?"

"I do not care enough about him to hate him. Nor pity him, as pitiful as he is. . . ."

David remained silent.

"He stopped me outside the company two days after you asked me to marry to tell me that he wanted me back. I told him that I had no desire to see him again. He called me a harlot and said that when I had the baby, it would be for the world to know, but that he knew of a way to take the child so that it would not interfere with our life together." MaryAnne grimaced as she turned away. "I have never wanted to hurt anyone in my life, but at that moment, I wanted to kill him. He just stared at me with this arrogant grin as if he had just rescued me from disrepute, as if I should fall to my knees in gratitude. I slapped him. I knew he would probably beat me again, even in public, but I didn't care.

"Just then, one of the clerks came around the corner.

I suspect that he had observed the exchange, as he stopped and asked if he could be of assistance. Virgil was mad with rage, but he is a coward. He raised a finger to me, sneered, then stormed off. That is his name. Virgil. It leaves a putrid taste in my mouth to even speak it."

She looked into David's eyes.

"Once I thought I loved him, but now he is irrelevant, David. To me, he is nothing, but more especially to Andrea. I beg you, as her father, not to tell her. It has no chance of bringing her happiness and may bring her great pain."

Her voice cracked. "The only question we should reason is how it will affect her happiness, is it not?"

David silently contemplated the question. Then his mouth rose in a half smile. "I love you, MaryAnne. I truly love you."

VIII

CHAPTER EIGHT

The Widow's Gift

"I find it most peculiar that these old women share their deepest secrets with a man who, but a few months previous, they would have shrunk from in terror had they encountered him on a streetcar."

DAVID PARKIN'S DIARY. AUGUST 1, 1911

n a strange twist of social convention, Lawrence had become the toast of the city's elite widowhood, and those who sought its ranks would drop his name at teas and brunches like a secret password. Initially, the elderly women had begun the visits to Lawrence's shack because it was perfectly scandalous and gave rise to gossip, but through time, the visits had evolved and now came more through loneliness than social pretension. It was suspected that some widows would actually damage their clocks as an excuse to visit the horologist.

Though the widows rarely left their homes after dark, as summer stretched the day, the visits would sometimes intrude upon Lawrence's dinner. This particular evening, Lawrence was cutting carrots into a pan with a steel buck knife when there came a familiar, sharp wooden rap at his door. He lifted the blackened pan from the stove and greeted the widow. Maud Cannon, a gaunt, gray-haired woman, stood outside, leaning against a black, pearl-embedded cane. She wore a maroon poplin dress with a satin sash and a gold maple-leaf-shaped brooch clipped to its bodice. In her left hand, she clutched a beaded purse. She was flanked by a knickered boy who strained beneath the weight of a large, bronze-statued clock.

"Lemme take that," Lawrence said, quickly stepping outside to relieve the boy of the clock, who surrendered it gratefully. "You go right on in, Miss Maud."

"Thank you, Lawrence." She turned to the boy. "You wait outside," she said sternly, then stepped inside ahead of Lawrence, who set the clock on the worktable, then returned with a cloth and dusted off the chair she stood by. Its surface was already clean, but this was an expected ritual and one not to be neglected.

"Sit down, ma'am."

"Thank you, Lawrence." She straightened herself up in the chair. "I would like the clock cleaned."

Lawrence's brow furled. "Somethin' wrong with the work I done last week, ma'am?"

The woman looked back at the clock, as a confused expression blanketed her face. She cleared her throat. "No, Lawrence, you always do a fine job. It is just that I have visitors calling this week and I would like the clock ware to be especially nice."

Lawrence had known the woman long enough to discern the truth. She had forgotten which clock she had last brought.

"You shore know how to entertain your guests, Miss Maud. They must appreciate your hospitality."

She sighed. "I do not think they even notice." She brought out an elaborately embroidered handkerchief and patted her brow. "I think the bell on that one sounds flat."

"I'll be shore to check that, Miss Maud." He opened the crystal door and pushed the long hand to the half hour. The bell struck once in perfect pitch. "Shore is a luv'ly piece, it's a right honor to work on her." He stepped back and admired the clock. "Seth 'n' Thomas makes a right luv'ly piece."

It was a white-faced clock surrounded by a pot-metal sculpture of an angel pointing heavenward, as a young girl clasps her hands to pray.

"You'd think that angel gonna fly right off there."

The widow smiled, patted her brow again, then replaced the handkerchief in her purse. "I have a special request of you, Lawrence."

"Yes, ma'am?"

"I would like to call you Larry."

He looked back at the widow. "Larry?"

"Yes, we've known each other for some time. Would that be acceptable to you?"

Lawrence cared little for the name but had no desire to offend his client. "I s'pose so, ma'am. Ain't no one ever called me Larry before."

"If it's all the same."

"Yes, ma'am."

She sat back contentedly. "Larry, lately I have been given to much thought about you. Maybe it is because of you being a Negro and not having much, but it seems to me that you are one of the few people I know who truly appreciates the value of things. Like this clock here," she said, gesturing toward the table. "That is why I can take my clocks to you without anxiety."

"Thank you, ma'am."

"Back when my Rodney was alive, bless his soul, he appreciated things. Rodney would look at a sunset like he had discovered the thing. You would think it was God's gift just for him." She sighed and her voice softened in longing. "How life turns. The only family I have now is my miserable nephew."

"Your nephew appreciate things, ma'am?"

She frowned. "My nephew's a damn fool. I should not curse, but it is the gospel truth. I give him money and he spends it on liquor and gaming and I shudder to think what else." She leaned forward. "He thinks when I die he will have a pretty sizable inheritance, but that will be over my dead body!" she said indignantly. Suddenly, her mouth twisted into an amused grin. "I suppose all inheritances are over a dead body, Larry."

"Yes, ma'am, I s'pose they are at that."

"I'm sure it will come as a surprise, but I am leaving every dime to the church missionary fund."

"Now don't you go talkin' about no dyin', ma'am."

The old lady sighed. "Larry, I am not fooling anyone. I haven't many sunrises left." Her voice suddenly turned tired and melancholy. "My friends are nearly all gone now. It's lonely here, Larry. I feel as if I am just waiting around." She leaned forward, shaking a willowy finger for emphasis. "Leave when they still want you, Rodney used to say." She looked down at the floor and her eyes blinked slowly. "I have stayed too long."

Lawrence could not help but feel sympathy for the old woman. "Don't no one know their time, Miss Maud. But it stops for all of us. Be right shore 'bout that."

She looked up. "You know, Larry, I enjoy our little visits. They are the sunshine of my week. When I go, I have a mind to leave you something." The idea brightened her face. "Yes. That rose-gold timepiece you think so much of."

"Ma'am, I can't go takin' no timepieces."

"It is a very special timepiece. It should go to someone who will appreciate it. I am sure it will cause a commotion, giving a piece of the family inheritance to a Negro, but I do not care. It feels kind of nice to be controversial at my age. I am going to have it written in my will."

"How 'bout your nephew?"

The woman humphed. "Damn fool. He'd pawn it for

liquor a half hour after it fell into his idle hands. Not another word, Larry, you must have it. I insist."

"S'pose I'd rather have your company, ma'am."

She smiled sadly and patted his hand. "That is not our choice, Larry. To be sure, I have not felt too well of late." She again produced the handkerchief from her purse and dabbed her cheeks. "I will be going now, Larry," she said feebly.

Lawrence rose first and helped the woman to her feet, handing her the ebony cane.

"Thank you, Larry."

"You're welcome, ma'am." Lawrence opened the door and gestured to the boy, who took the widow's arm and helped her back to her carriage.

◆

"It is a question worthy of the philosophers—do we have dreams or do dreams have us? Myself, I do not believe in the mystical or prophetic nature of dreams. But I may be mistaken."

DAVID PARKIN'S DIARY. MARCH 17, 1912

Two hours before sunrise, MaryAnne woke with a start and began sobbing heavily into the mattress. She was having difficulty catching her breath. David sat up alarmed. "What is it, MaryAnne?"

"Oh, David!" she exclaimed. "It all seemed so real! So horribly real!"

"What, Mary?"

She buried her head into his chest and began to cry. "I had the most awful dream."

David put his arms around her.

"I dreamt I was in bed nursing Andrea when an angel came in through the window, took her from my breast, then flew out with her."

David pulled her tight. "It was only a dream, Mary."

She wiped the tears from her face with the sleeve of her gown. "I must see her."

"I will go," David said. He climbed out of bed and walked the length of the hall to the nursery. Andrea lay motionless, her cheek painted in moonlit strokes. She suddenly rolled over to her side and David exhaled in relief. He quickly returned to the bedroom. "She is fine. She is sleeping fine." He wearily climbed back into the bed.

"Do you think it meant something?" MaryAnne asked.

"I don't think so. We always dream our greatest fears," David said reassuringly.

MaryAnne sniffed. "I'm sorry I woke you."

He kissed her forehead, then lay back with his arm around her and pulled her close. "Good night."

"Good night, David." MaryAnne cuddled up next to him and eventually fell back asleep. David stared sleeplessly at the ceiling.

◆

The following morning, MaryAnne walked into the nursery and pulled back the drapery, filling the room with virgin sunlight.

"Good morning, sweet Andrea," she sang lightly. She sat down on the bed. "Time to wake up." Andrea opened her eyes slowly. Her eyelids were heavy and swollen. Her lips were dry and cracked.

"Andrea?"

"Mama, my neck hurts."

MaryAnne lay her cheek across Andrea's forehead and instantly pulled back. She was hot with fever. She ran to the doorway and called for Catherine, who appeared almost instantly.

"Andrea is feverish, fetch me some wet rags and ice from the box. Send Mark with the carriage for Dr. Bouk."

"Yes, ma'am," she said, running off. MaryAnne knelt by the bed and stroked Andrea's forehead. A few mo-

ments later, Catherine, quite out of breath, returned
with the articles.

MaryAnne took the cloth, wrapped it around the ice
and held it up against Andrea's forehead. For the first
time, she noticed the rash across her cheek. The night's
dream echoed back to her in haunting remembrance.
She quickly pushed it away.

Andrea had fallen back to sleep by the time Mark returned with the carriage. Catherine quickly led the doctor up to the nursery. Dr. Bouk had been David's personal
physician ever since David first came to the city and
was no stranger to the Parkin household. As he entered
the room, MaryAnne moved to the opposite side of the
bed. He was of a serious demeanor and acknowledged
MaryAnne with a simple nod. "Mrs. Parkin."

"Doctor, she has a fever and a rash."

He set his leather bag on the ground and bent over
the child. He placed his hands on the sides of Andrea's
neck and lifted his forefingers beneath her jaw. "Does
that hurt, sweetheart?" Andrea nodded lethargically.
He frowned, then gently opened the child's mouth.
Her tongue was white, with fine red marks.

"It is scarlatina," he said slowly. "The scarlet fever."

The pronouncement sent chills through MaryAnne.

There had already been eighteen deaths in the city that year from the disease. She wrung her hands. Catherine moved next to her.

"What do I do?"

Doctor Bouk stood up and removed his bifocals. He was a tall, gangly man, emaciatingly thin, with an ironic pouch of a stomach. "She must stay in bed, of course. Within a few days, the rash may become dusky. I will administer an ointment that will help stop the spread of the disease. It should make her more comfortable." He reached into his bag, then lifted out a small vial. "This is biniodide of mercury. I will give her a half grain. It may arrest the fever and prevent the desquamation—the skin flaking off." He raised his hand to his mouth and coughed. "A daily hot salt or mustard bath may help. Glycerin and water will aid the throat. Catherine, you can get the glycerin from an apothecary. It should be administered directly to the inside of the throat."

"How long does the illness last?"

The doctor frowned. "Maybe forty days—with good fortune."

He did not need to explain. MaryAnne knew that death often occurred within the first two weeks.

"Be of good cheer, Mrs. Parkin. There have not been

as many deaths from scarlet fever as there were before the century." He stood up and touched her shoulder, then stopped at the door. "I must notify the city health department. They will quarantine your home."

MaryAnne nodded. "Of course," she said. When he was gone, she sat down on the bed, fighting back the tears that gathered. Catherine put her arm around her.

"Where is David?"

"He is coming, MaryAnne. Mark went to fetch him."

MaryAnne looked down on her resting child. Catherine brushed back MaryAnne's hair.

"My brother got the fever two summers ago," she said, hoping to console her mistress. "He is fine now."

"What did you do?"

"My mama dipped bacon in coal oil and laid it on his head and throat."

MaryAnne wiped her eyes. "That is all?"

"We prayed over him."

"Your brother was healed?"

"He is weaker of constitution, but he is recovered."

She turned away from the child and spoke in hushed and desperate tones. "I will do anything, Catherine."

Catherine embraced her tighter.

"Anything, but lose her."

◆

That afternoon, the local health officer quarantined the home, posting on the doorway a large China-red placard that read QUARANTINE. The following weeks languished with MaryAnne sitting by Andrea's side. Each day was a carbon copy of the previous one, the one exception being MaryAnne, who appeared more haggard and frail with each passing day. By the end of the second week, she looked gaunt, her eyes encircled by dark rings, and her skin was waxen. She spoke infrequently and, to Catherine, seemed to be caught up in some fearful trance. David's concern for his wife grew until it equaled that which he felt for Andrea. Scarlet fever was uncommon in adults, but not unheard of, especially in someone as weakened as MaryAnne had become. David looked in on her with increasing frequency and anxiety until he could bear her vigil no longer. That night, he brought the dinners into the room himself. He set the tray down, then brushed the hair back from Andrea's forehead as she slept.

"MaryAnne, Catherine tells me you have not left Andrea's side all week."

She didn't reply, but took the bowl of clear soup. David observed that she moved slowly, as if her muscles had grown weak. He frowned. "Come, MaryAnne. Come out into the day. I will watch after Andrea."

She did not respond.

"MaryAnne!"

"I cannot leave her, David."

"You must!"

She shook her head.

David felt himself growing angry with her stubbornness. "This is madness, MaryAnne. Why can you not leave her?"

She looked up at him, her eyes filled with pain. She whispered, "What if I never got to say good-bye?"

David gazed back into MaryAnne's deep, fatigued eyes. "Will it come to that?"

She set the bowl down and leaned into him, looking down at her little girl. "It mustn't. It mustn't."

◆

"Is this life, to grasp joy only to fear its escape?
The price of happiness is the risk of losing it."

DAVID PARKIN'S DIARY. APRIL 3, 1912

It was a Wednesday morning that MaryAnne woke to the sound of laughter. Andrea was sitting up in her bed laughing at the mockingbird that pecked at the windowsill.

Doubting her senses, MaryAnne rose slowly and moved over to the child. She touched Andrea's forehead.

"Andrea. Are you well?"

The little girl beamed up at her mother. "Did you see the bird?" Her eyes, though still heavy from a month of sickness, were bright and color had returned to the previously ashen skin.

MaryAnne called for David, who, fearing the worst, quickly entered the room with Catherine following behind him. He was surprised to see the child sitting upright.

"I can't believe it."

Catherine clapped. "Oh, MaryAnne!"

"David, she is well! Andrea is well!"

David walked over to the bed.

"Hi, Papa. Did you see the bird?"

David looked to the window. "He has flown away. Did he say anything to you?"

"Birds don't talk."

"I forgot," he said whimsically.

He kissed her on the forehead, then turned back to

MaryAnne and took her in his arms. "You did it, Mary. By sheer will, or love, you won."

◆

The next day, before the clocks of the Parkin home had proclaimed the tenth hour, Lawrence limped up the cobblestone drive to the mansion, his broad-rimmed felt hat bent against the morning sun. In one hand swung a book.

Catherine stood on the porch polishing the paned windows in curt, rectangular swipes. She turned around when she saw Lawrence's reflection.

"Good morning, Mr. Flake."

Lawrence tipped his hat. "Mornin', Miss Catherine. Is David or Miss MaryAnne 'bout?"

Just then MaryAnne, who had seen him approach, stepped outside. "Lawrence, welcome."

"Miss MaryAnne!" Lawrence's expression betrayed his surprise at how emaciated she had become.

MaryAnne blushed. "I'm sorry, I must look frightful."

"No, ma'am," Lawrence replied quickly, "you look as pretty as you always done."

MaryAnne smiled at the kind fib. "It's been a hard time, Lawrence."

"I know, ma'am. And you been a rock." Lawrence lowered his hat, relegating it to the same hand which held the book. He scratched his head. "I was thinkin' that maybe with the fever gone I could see Andrea. I brought her a book, thought maybe I could read to her."

"Of course you may. She would love that. Please come in." MaryAnne led him up to the nursery and announced the visitor to Andrea, who happily bounced up in bed, shedding the tied quilt that covered her legs.

"Hi, Lawrence!"

"How you feelin', missy?" Lawrence asked, stepping into the dusky room.

"You can come in. I'm not sick!"

"Your mama told me you feelin' much better."

MaryAnne smiled at the exchange, then excusing herself, shut the door behind them. Lawrence sat down on the edge of the small bed next to her and displayed the book. "I came to read you a story."

"What's it about?"

"It's 'bout a rabbit."

"I know a story about a rabbit that got into a farmer's garden."

"Well, this, missy, is a story 'bout a rabbit made of velveteen. You know what velveteen is?"

She shook her head.

"Velveteen is somethin' real soft, like this blanket here. Feels good against your face." As he said this, he gently stroked her cheek with his forefinger. Andrea grinned accusingly.

"Your finger's not soft."

He held up his hands in easy surrender. "These hands done too much work to be soft."

She looked at the aged, scarred hands. "Lawrence, will I turn brown when I get old?"

Lawrence broke out in laughter. "No, missy, you won't be turnin' brown." He rubbed her head. "We best get us some more light if we gonna read." He drew back the curtains so that a beam of sunlight fell across the bed and climbed the opposite wall. He began the story, carefully holding the book so that Andrea could see its brightly illustated pages. She was captivated by the tale and spoke only once: when he had committed the unpardonable crime of turning the page before she was done looking at the picture. A half hour later he announced the story's end and lay the book in his lap.

"That boy had what I had," Andrea said. "Scarly-fever."

"And you got better jus' like him."

She nodded. "I like that rabbit. Can we read it again?"

"I told your mama that I wouldn't be too long. Don't want to disturb your nap time."

The child frowned.

"I'll leave the book so you can look at the pictures," he said, holding the book out to her.

Andrea smiled as she accepted the offering. "I'm glad you turned brown, Lawrence."

"Why's that, missy?"

"Because I'll always know it's you."

Lawrence pulled the blanket up over her shoulders as she nestled up against his knee. He leaned over and kissed her on the forehead, then pulled the curtains tight as the room fell back into a silent infirmary.

As he left the home he noticed that someone had removed the red placard from the front porch.

◆

"The most consequential of life's episodes often begin with the simplest of events."

DAVID PARKIN'S DIARY. OCTOBER 15, 1913

Lawrence thought the widows peculiar about death. He learned of Maud Cannon's passing through another widow, who gossiped cavalierly about the small turn-out at Maud's wake.

A few days later, there was a knock at Lawrence's door. A man, dressed in a brown-striped suit and carrying a leather valise, stood outside his shack. He was a pale man with oiled, combed-back hair and pocked skin. His left eye twitched nervously.

"Mr. Flake?"

"Yessuh."

"Mr. Lawrence Flake?"

Lawrence nodded.

He stared at the black man. "Do you have identification papers?"

"I know who I am," Lawrence said defiantly.

The lawyer rubbed his chin. "Yes." He set down his case, reached into his pocket and produced a small package. An aged jeweler's box with a vermilion crushed-velvet veneer. He handed Lawrence the box.

"Needs repairin'?"

"No. It belongs to you. Our client, the late Maud Cannon, specified in her will that this was to be endowed to you."

"You her nephew?"

"I am the executor of the will," he replied indignantly. "She wanted you to have this jewelry. Now, if you will please sign this paper, I will go."

Lawrence glanced up from the gift. He took the pen and signed the document, wherein the man disappeared as promised. Lawrence stepped back inside, extracted the watch from its case, and held it up to the light, smiling at the exquisite rose-gold timepiece. "Thank you, Miss Maud," he said aloud. He set the watch back in its case and went back to his paper.

◆

At first David thought the gunshot was the coughing backfire of his Pierce Arrow. He had concluded the day's business early and as Lawrence had recently received consignment of the estate of a former steel tycoon known for his eccentricities and remarkable antiques, David thought to stop by to examine the former magnate's possessions.

He pulled his car up the dirt drive alongside the east brick wall of the cannery, parking beneath a large painted advertisement expounding the virtues of Schoals shoe black. The car coughed twice before the discharge of a firearm echoed loudly in the back lot, followed by a faint cry. It sounded as if it had come from Lawrence's shack.

Apprehensively, David sprinted around to the back of the building. He found the door to Lawrence's shack wide open. He cautiously peered inside. On the wood-planked floor a small man with a thick reddish beard lay on his back in a pool of dark liquid. The smell of whiskey reeked over the sharp stench of ignited gun powder.

On the wooden tabletop lay a Winchester rifle. Lawrence sat on the floor in the corner of the room, his eyes vacuous, as if waiting for something he was powerless to stop. He was moaning softly. "Oh Lordy, oh Lordy."

"Lawrence, what has happened here?"

Lawrence stared straight ahead.

"Lawrence?"

Lawrence slowly looked up. He extended a clenched fist, then opened it to expose the delicate rose-gold wristwatch. The widow's gift.

"Man I ain't never see before pushed his way into my home screamin' no nigger gonna take his watch. Called me a thief, voodoo-witch doctor. Sez I put a spell on the widow to make her give it to me."

David looked down at the dead man.

"He was stinkin' drunk. Started a-shovin' me with his gun. I sez, 'You take the watch, I ain't never asked for no watch.' Made him crazier. Sez, 'You think this watch is yours to give, nigger? Think I need some nigger tell me what's rightfully mine?' Started into cryin', sez his aunt loves a nigger more than her own flesh. Tha's when he lifted his gun. I been in war. I know the look in a man's eyes when he's gonna kill."

Lawrence closed his hand around the timepiece. His face was hard, yet fearful, creased in deep flesh canyons. "Ain't no watch he wanted."

Just then, there was a sharp, metallic click behind them—the bolt action of a carbine. The door opened and a thin man with red cheeks and small puffy eyes stepped into the room. He wore a navy blue, double-breasted police uniform with gold buttons and a black velvet collar and a bell-shaped hat with a diminutive leather rim. He held a rifle chest-high and his eyes darted nervously between David, Lawrence, and the dead man.

"Stand up, Negro.

Lawrence pushed himself up against the wall. The officer knelt down and placed his fingers on the man's throat. "Everen, you jackass. So you finally got yours," he said to the corpse. He looked up.

"Who killed this man?"

"I did," David said.

The officer stood back up. He looked at the firearm on the table. "Whose gun is that?"

David gestured towards the lifeless body. "It's his. I killed him with his own gun."

The officer noted the look of astonishment on Lawrence's face. He pointed his rifle at David. "You come with me."

"You won't need the gun."

The sheriff turned towards Lawrence. "You come too."

"He doesn't have anything to do with this," David protested.

"This your home, Negro?"

"Yessuh."

"You see this man get shot?"

Lawrence glanced over at David. "Yessuh."

"Then you have something to do with this. Come along."

A crowd of onlookers had already gathered outside the shack as the two men were led to the horse-drawn paddy wagon and driven off to jail.

◆

The police captain stared at David over a desk cluttered with papers and a dinner of baked chicken, black beans, and Apple Brown Betty. He suddenly smiled. "Mr. Parkin, please sit down." He motioned to an austere wooden chair. "Please."

The sudden display of courtesy struck David as rather peculiar and he speculated that someone in authority had called on his behalf.

"Care for anything?" He gestured towards a platter. "Saratoga potatoes?"

David looked at the food and shook his head.

"I just heard from the mayor's office, Mr. Parkin. The mayor wishes to express his personal concern with this matter and hopes that you have been treated respectfully."

"I have no complaints."

"He personally vouches for your character and wishes to see you sent on your way. In light of Officer Brookes's report, and your reputation, I see no reason to further detain you."

David looked back at the door. "Then I am free to go?"

"Certainly. I am curious, though. Do you know the man that was killed?"

"No."

"Everen Hatt. He was a regular down here. Everyone in this building, including the domestics, know him by sight." He leaned forward onto his thick hands. "This affair ought to be very clear, Mr. Parkin. Hatt was a brawler and a drunk. He was shot in someone else's residence. The only weapon that was discharged was his. What I don't understand is your testimony that you shot the man."

"Why is that difficult?"

He leaned back, picking his teeth with his thumb. "Witnesses claim they saw you enter the shack after the gunshot."

"They must be mistaken."

The police captain looked at him in disbelief. "Yes . . ." His expression suddenly turned grave. "A word of caution, Mr. Parkin. In spite of your connections, these are serious matters. A man has been killed. There will be an inquest and no doubt a hearing." He pushed his chair back from his desk. "I don't know what this Negro has on you, but I hope to heaven it does not go bad. "

David ignored the warning. "May I go now?"

"You are free to leave." The Captain shook a brass desk bell and the officer reappeared at the doorway.

"Brookes, kindly take Mr. Parkin back to his automobile."

"What about my friend?" David asked.

He rubbed his nose. "And release the Negro."

"Yes, sir."

"And, Brookes, shut the door."

"Yes, sir."

When the door had shut, the captain leaned forward to a cold dinner and cursed the mayor for his interference in the affair.

◆

MaryAnne had just heard of David's arrest and was preparing to go to him when he entered the front door.

"David! Are you all right?"

David looked at her blankly. "I will be in my den," he said as he walked past her. Catherine smiled at Mary-Anne sympathetically. MaryAnne took her hand. "It will be all right," she said.

An hour later, she entered David's den carrying a silver-plated tea service. Two sconces lit the wall, teasing the darkness with flickering illumination. From outside, the din of crickets sang in syncopated harmony to the voices of the clocks in the room.

"I thought you might like some tea. And perhaps some company."

He looked up and smiled. "I am sorry. I did not mean to ignore you."

She handed him a cup, then set the tray on a buffet and sat on the love seat next to him. "Are you all right?"

"Yes. I am fine."

She hesitated, gathering courage for her question. "David. Why did you tell them that you shot the man?"

"You do not believe that I did?"

"I do not believe you are capable of killing a man."

David stared vacantly into space. The room was quiet and MaryAnne looked at him pensively.

"It seems unlikely to me that Lawrence would get a fair trial."

"Mark told me the police officer said that this was a very clear case of self-defense."

"Lawrence did not have the mayor vouching for him. If it was Lawrence on trial that clear case would suddenly become very murky." David frowned. "Even if he was acquitted, the man's family would likely lynch Lawrence for a miscarriage of justice, not because he was guilty, but because he is a Negro. The only way to protect Lawrence is to keep him out of it."

"What if they want to lynch you?"

David thought for a moment. He had not considered this possibility. "A man cannot live his life by the calculations of retribution. I did what I had to do and hope the consequences are kind."

"You are a good man, David. I pray that God will be good to us in this matter."

"I am disinclined to think God takes notice of such things."

MaryAnne took a sip of tea. "Then you believe it a mere coincidence that you arrived when you did?"

David found the query intriguing. "I had not considered it. I don't know, MaryAnne. I really do not know if God or fate meddles in our affairs."

"It seems to me that there is a 'divinity that shapes our ends.' "

David contemplated the assertion. "If this is true, then you must accept that this God, or fate, also besets our species with great calamities."

"It is our lot . . ." MaryAnne replied solemnly. She set down her cup. "I cannot answer for the whole of human suffering. I can only speak from my experience. But I have found that my pain is instructive. That through it I become more than I would otherwise."

David considered her argument. "To become . . ." He rubbed his forehead. "I think oftentimes that instruction is too hard to bear." He looked at his wife, then smiled in surrender. "I have become much too serious in my matrimonial state. And perhaps fatalistic. If that same divinity has brought you across the sea to me then it must be of some good."

"Or at least have good humor," she said, suddenly laughing at her husband. She kissed his cheek and laughed again.

David lay back in the plush seat. "Oh, MaryAnne, that laughter. How I need it."

"Then you shall have it." MaryAnne fell laughing into his arms as David covered her face with kisses.

◆

"I confess that I find it difficult to take this affair seriously, and were it not for MaryAnne's anxiety, I would, perhaps, not concern myself with it at all."

DAVID PARKIN'S DIARY. NOVEMBER 22, 1913

David received notice of the trial two weeks after his arrest and regarded it with little more concern than a coal bill. The trial had been set for the third of December and though it was not of any great interest to David, it provided ample fodder for the local tabloids, which increased circulation with sensational headlines: LOCAL MILLIONAIRE TRIED FOR MURDER.

The city became caught up in the scandal and nowhere more so than at the bar Everen Hatt had frequented with his soul mate and mentor, Cal Barker.

Everen Hatt's disposition could not be blamed entirely on Barker. Hatt was a self-made loser even before he met the man; a year after Hatt's parents died and he was taken in by his only living relative, the wealthy widow Maud Cannon. The widow learned with great distress of the shallowness of her nephew's character and, with Christian resolve, set about to reform the boy, leading to squabbles that increased daily in frequency and rancor. It was months before she began to learn the extent of his depravity. He readily took from her with no thought of gratitude or obligation, and when she finally refused to further finance his incessant drinking, valuables began to disappear from around the house. She confronted him with the losses, to which he responded so violently that she feared for her safety and never mentioned the subject again, quietly hiding the pieces with the greatest sentimental value. So when a few years later he begged a sizable stipend with the promise that he would leave her life forever, she gave him the money and considered it a small price to rid him from her life. Not surprisingly, he was not true to the arrangement and descended upon her at least twice a year for additional subsidy.

So it was for nearly a decade. Hatt had enjoyed a sense of celebrity among his friends as a relative of the rich, with an occasional allowance to prove it. As the widow's only relative, he, and Barker, erroneously assumed that Hatt would be the only heir of her estate and fantasized about the day when the old lady would die and they would live a glorious lifestyle of unlimited gratification. The fantasies filled the men briefly with delusions of wealth, but left them all the hungrier at the reality of their present circumstance.

Growing increasingly impatient with the woman's longevity, Barker had offered to hasten the happy occasion by helping the widow on her way. It was not a surprise to anyone that Barker would make such an offer. Cal Barker lived his life in darkness. As a miner, his days were spent in the belly of the earth and his nights on the darker parts of its surface.

He was married, though there was little evidence of

his marital status, and he returned home just often enough to force himself on his wife, a plain-faced woman who feared the large man and tacitly accepted his abuse and neglect. She had borne four children which she provided the sustenance for through hiring herself out for domestic chores and occasionally from what was left of Barker's wages after the gambling and alcohol had taken its due.

Barker's life of darkness was more than one of locale. He lived his life in sole pursuit of its baser desires, discovering that pleasures diminish with indulgence and become harder to come by. And as those who chase the unattainable do, he grew meaner with age. Mean enough to kill a widow.

Hatt, on the other hand, though unfettered by moral turpitude, feared the possibility of a noose. "She's an old-enough bag of bones," he told Barker. "Ain't hardly got another year left in her. Let God do the dirty work."

◆

The day the widow died, there were two rounds of drinks on Hatt, which exhausted the last of his money, followed by another from Barker, who was sure to share in Hatt's good fortune. Not coincidentally, his register of friends swelled that day, and Hatt, who had never enjoyed such eminence, was just stupid enough to believe in his new-found popularity.

Six days later, at the reading of the widow's last will and testament, Hatt's dreams were shattered. It was fortunate for all present that Hatt had not brought a gun into the law office, as he would likely have killed all present, then turned the weapon on himself.

Once the initial shock of the reading wore off, the details of the will became of greater concern to the men. They found that the bulk of the estate was willed to a church—a faceless entity in which their only retribution lay in profaning God, something they had long before perfected. Then, a week later, Wallace Schoefield, one of the better readers of the group, stumbled onto the one individual who had received a personal gift. A golden timepiece had been bestowed upon a man by the name of Lawrence Flake. Upon further investigation, they discovered that the man was a Negro— a revelation that only added to their outrage.

In the twisted reasoning of the unjust (that all things which do not incur to their benefit are inherently unfair), the men decided that the timepiece was rightfully theirs and that they would claim it at any cost.

Hatt's motivations ran deeper. He was, as the widow ascertained, unable to derive gratification from anything of true value in life and, frustrated at his own character, despised all those who could. And this was Hatt's state of mind when he went after the delicate golden wristwatch, when in reality he wanted nothing more than to kill the man upon whom it was endowed.

◆

The trial began at exactly nine in the morning, presided over by the Honorable William G. Halloran—an old man rarely seen outside a courtroom, who dressed spartanly and viewed justice and wardrobe with the same idiosyncratic fervor.

Due to the sensationalism of the trial, the gallery was filled to capacity and spectators stood against the wall and outer doors. The press was well represented and had secured many of the better seats near the front of the courtroom or against the wall near the oak jury box, where hats were hung in a row.

The twelve-man jury wore stone faces throughout

the ordeal, listening to the arguments dutifully. By six o'clock, it was over. The jury unanimously found Hatt guilty of trespassing with intent to kill and that David, a model citizen, had acted in self-defense.

Despite the tabloids' promise of a good show, by the end of the trial few were surprised at the reading of the verdict, and the only excitement of the day came when a juror, taking aim at a spittoon, inadvertently nailed a constable, who reacted by brandishing a billy club over the man.

At the conclusion of the reading, the judge thanked the jury for their service and dismissed them, while MaryAnne breathed a great sigh of relief and embraced Catherine, who sat next to her in the gallery. The four adult members of the Parkin household joined outside the courtroom and all seemed exceptionally relieved except David, who had never shared their anxiety.

"I had expected more of a show."

"I will not say I am disappointed," MaryAnne said. "I am just happy it is all over."

"I am happy that I have not lost all of the day," David replied, lifting a gold pocket watch from his vest pocket. "I need to meet with Gibbs. Mark, see the ladies on home. I will walk to the office."

"Shall I come for you later?"

"Gibbs will bring me home."

"Hurry back," MaryAnne urged.

"Always, my love."

David kissed her twice, once for Andrea, and they parted company. He entered the narrow alleyway next to the courthouse and hurried off to his office. As he neared the end of the passage, three men blocked his path. David recognized one of them from the courtroom.

"Excuse me," he said, expecting and receiving little reaction from the men.

The largest of the men, Cal Barker, stepped forward and struck David across the face, knocking him backward. David rubbed his cheek, then, lowering his hand, noticed the blood on his fingers. Again, Barker sprang forward. This time, he grabbed David by the jacket and shoved him up against the yellow brick of the nearby building. His breath reeked of cheap whiskey.

"They say that you had nuthin' to do with Hatt's murder, that the nigger killed Hatt."

David said nothing.

"A white man coverin' for a nigger. Whatsa matter with you?"

David remained silent, staring at Barker dispassion-
ately. The man's face turned crimson.

"You stinkin' rich, think you can buy anything. Well,
you can't buy justice. We'll get our justice."

David's face showed no sign of intimidation, which
only provoked Barker further. "Whatsa matter with
you! You dumb?! Don't you know I could kill you right
now?"

Confusing control with cowardice, Barker awk-
wardly recoiled to strike David again. David quickly
swung around, slamming his fist against the bridge of
Barker's nose and knocking him up against the opposite
wall. Barker let out a small cry, then slumped to the
ground. The two standing men moved toward David.
David flashed a slim black ten-shooter from his waist-
coat and leveled it at Barker.

"Back off! And you stay down or you will die like Hatt."

Barker motioned to the men with his eyes and they
retreated. Barker wiped at the thin stream of blood that
flowed from his nose.

"You are not the ass your appearance would suggest."
He looked up at the two men, continuing to point the
gun at Barker's head.

"Step aside."

The men moved to the wall. As David made his escape, Barker spat blood on the ground and scowled.
"Justice will be served, Parker. We will have justice."

"Parker? It's Parkin, you ass."

◆

At David's arrival, Gibbs slid the bolt from the door
and let him in, then barred it behind them. He noticed
the blood on David's hands and chin.

"What happened?"

"Hatt's friends."

Without explanation, David went up to his office
with Gibbs following closely behind. He set a lit candle on his desk, then reclined in his chair, rubbing his
fist. Gibbs sat down in the chair before his desk.

"What are you going to do?"

"About what?"

"These hoodlums."

David shrugged. "Nothing. It's done."

Gibbs leaned forward toward the desk. "David, listen to me. There is much talk about these men. It's not
going to end here. They are trouble."

David stared quietly at the candle burning on the table. A wax tear fell to its base. He looked up slowly. "What would you have me do? The trial is done."

"Go back. Turn Lawrence over to the law. Let him go to trial."

David looked at him levelly. "What kind of trial?"

"What does it matter! If they hang him, they hang him! He's an old man, a poor old man! He's got nothing, David, you've got your whole life ahead of you."

"What kind of life could that be knowing that I had betrayed a friend?"

"Betrayed?" His eyes squinted in disbelief. "He put himself in this situation, not you! David . . . he's a Negro!"

David looked at him sadly, then dropped his head in his hands. He felt weary. "Leave me, please."

Gibbs sighed, then reluctantly stood. "We have been through a lot together and you always seem to come out on top. But I have a bad feeling about this. I grant you that what you are doing is noble in its own way, but the cost of what you are doing is too great."

David shook his head. "No, Gibbs. Only the cost of doing nothing is ever too great."

◆

"All is ashes . . ."

It was easy for the five hooded men to enter Lawrence's shack. The structure had been constructed by the cannery as a storage shed, so it could not be locked from the inside but only from the exterior by a rusted steel latch that had once run horizontally across the outside of the door. Lawrence had removed the latch the previous summer after some teens, in a schoolyard prank, had locked him in his own house. He had never considered moving the lock inside, thinking to himself, *Who would rob a shack?*

The men entered clumsily, growling in foul and guttural tones, drunk with whiskey and hatred. They hovered above the sleeping man only long enough to focus their assault. Lawrence was awakened by the rifle butt that smashed across his face. Panicked and bleary-eyed, he looked up at the hooded men who stood over him. Suddenly, one of them struck him across the face with a metal flask, then fell on him, thrashing wildly. With a powerful kick, Lawrence sent the man sprawling backward into a pile of clocks. In an instant, three men pounced on him, pummeling him with their fists, leaving his face a bloody mask. One clumsily tried to force a glass bottle into his mouth, which cut open his lip and cracked his front tooth, but slipped from the bumbling hands and bounded onto the floor and was lost in the darkness, followed by the man's cursing.

Lawrence managed to free one hand and, swinging wildly, knocked one of the men to the ground. His mind reeled in confusion. He did not know who was attacking him, nor what he could have done to warrant the assault.

As he struggled to raise himself, an ax handle caught him across the back of his head, knocking him off his cot and to the ground, unconscious. The men, growing increasingly sadistic in their violence, stripped him of his clothes, dragged him outside, and bound him to a tree, where they beat and kicked him until they thought him dead. Two of the men returned to the shack and, after taking what they had come for, smashed several clocks with the ax handle, then disappeared into the night.

◆

The fire spread quickly from the back porch, climbing upward to the second level, hungrily devouring all in its path. MaryAnne awoke to the baying of a mongrel dog and thought there was something peculiar about the dawn light shimmering through the bedroom window. Suddenly, there was a sharp crack, like the vaporous expansion of a log in the fireplace. She bolted up in bed as a thin stream of smoke snaked upward from beneath the bedroom door. "David! Our house is on fire!" She suddenly shrieked, "Andrea!"

David jumped up from the bed in horror. "Andrea! Dear God!"

David shot to the door and threw it open. A black pillow of smoke billowed into the room. The end of the hallway was completely engulfed in flames and from behind the wall of fire came a horrible sound. Andrea's cry.

MaryAnne screamed. "Andrea!"

"Mama!" Andrea wailed faintly from behind the flames.

David ran back to the bed and pulling a quilt over himself, pushed toward the inferno surrounding Andrea's room only to be repelled by the intense heat. He screamed out in frustration. The flames snapped fiercely, drowning out Andrea's pleas. Just then, another male voice hollered out. "David!" Mark raced up the stairs. "David!"

"Andrea is in the nursery! Alert the fire station!"

"Catherine has left to pull the alarm."

"Take MaryAnne out. I will climb the back railing to Andrea. Go!"

Outside, the pneumatic siren of a fire truck crescendoed as it entered the yard. A second fire vehicle, a large bell-shaped water drum drawn by horses, pulled into the yard behind it. The corps sprang to action. Two men began operating a pump hooked to the vehicle while a half dozen others, carrying leather fire buckets, streamed into the house, throwing water down the hallway.

In the yard below, Mark held MaryAnne back from her home. She sobbed and wrung her hands violently, each second weighing longer than the next. Where was David? Suddenly, he stumbled from the front doorway, coughing violently, his face streaked wet and blackened from smoke and soot. In his arms lay a motionless child.

CHAPTER NINE

The Release

"I know not why I am compelled to write at this time except as those caught in a torrent seek the surer ground and those caught in life's tempests seek the familiar and the mundane."

DAVID PARKIN'S DIARY. DECEMBER 4, 1913

hrough the heroic efforts of the fire corps, the fire had been isolated to the east wing, though the stench of smoke permeated the entire mansion. The house itself had escaped serious structural damage, but the damage inflicted upon its occupants was of far greater consequence.

Night had fallen and the drawing room was illuminated by the yellow radiance of kerosene sconces. Usually by this hour Catherine would have extinguished the wicks and secured the downstairs. Tonight, however, there was company in the house. The police officer rose when David entered the room.

"Mr. Parkin, I am Officer Brookes. Perhaps you remember me from the other day."

David habitually nodded.

"How is your daughter?" he asked cautiously.

"She is badly burned," David replied, his eyes betraying the emotion within.

"I'm truly sorry. I have a little one at home scarcely older than yours." The policeman paused. Then he continued, "It is our belief that the fire was deliberately set."

David said nothing. Just then, Catherine entered the room. She walked up to David and whispered in his ear. David turned toward her, anticipating some change in Andrea's condition.

Catherine read his intent. "There is no change, sir."

"I am needed upstairs," David said. "The doctor . . ."

Brookes frowned. "I am terribly sorry and I will leave you shortly but, please, just two questions."

David looked at the officer impatiently.

"I understand that yesterday you were threatened by a man named Cal Barker."

"I don't know the man's name."

"I was alerted yesterday about the confrontation in the alley, but I arrived too late. I found Barker at a bar and questioned him. He had a broken nose and was raving like a lunatic, but denied the incident. What were his words to you?"

David breathed out. "He said something about getting his own justice."

The officer nodded. "Barker was a friend of Everen Hatt's. I will be arresting him this afternoon. I will keep you informed." He stood up to go. "I am heartfelt sorry to intrude on you now, but time is of the essence. God bless your little one."

David glanced over at Catherine, who was waiting anxiously.

"I will see you to the door, Officer Brookes," Catherine said.

"I would be obliged."

David mumbled a thank-you, then climbed the stairs to the parlor, where Andrea was being cared for. Dr. Bouk stood outside the door, grim-faced and fatigued.

"She has not stirred yet," he said directly, as if in answer to an unspoken question. "If I thought she could survive the move, I would transport her to the hospital." He took a deep breath, then looked David in the eyes. "The child cannot possibly live."

David turned from the doctor and peered in through the crack in the parlor door to where MaryAnne knelt at the side of the walnut-framed bed. It was the same bed and room where she had given birth to Andrea three and a half years previous. The moment seemed frozen, betrayed only by the faint sound of a mantel clock. David turned to the doctor again. His eyes pled for solace. "Is there nothing to be done?"

The doctor frowned, nodding his head slowly. "The burns are too severe. She is running a high fever from the wounds." He removed his bifocals and rubbed the bridge of his nose. "I am very sorry, David. I wish I could give you hope. If she were conscious, she would be in excruciating pain." He returned his glasses to his shirt pocket and untied his apron. "Frankly, I do not know what is keeping her alive."

David looked back in at MaryAnne, bowed fervently over the bed, her cheek pressed against the feather mattress with her forehead touching Andrea's motionless torso.

"I know what is keeping her alive," he said softly.

The doctor frowned again, then removed his vesture. "If there were anything else I could do." He shook his head helplessly. "I'm sorry, David."

David looked down and said nothing as the physician departed. A moment later, David took a deep breath, then grasped the handle and gently pushed the door open, wide enough to enter. MaryAnne did not stir or acknowledge his entrance.

Across the room, the mechanical operation of MaryAnne's grandfather's clock stirred, its hammer ground into position, then, once set, chimed the quarter hour. David walked to the bed and knelt down behind MaryAnne, wrapping his arms around her waist. He laid his head against her back.

"MaryAnne," he whispered softly.

She did not respond. Across the room, the clock allowed its serpentine hand to advance another minute.

"MaryAnne . . ."

"No, David." Her voice was hoarse. "Please . . ."

His eyes moistened. "You must let her go, Mary."

MaryAnne closed her eyes tightly and swallowed. Only the sound of the clock's oscillating pendulum tore at the silence.

"She is my baby, David."

"Andrea will always be your baby, my love." He took a deep breath. "She will forever be our baby."

MaryAnne raised her head and looked on her daughter. Andrea's hair was spread against the pillow, wet at the roots from fever.

With the back of her hand, MaryAnne caressed Andrea's ruddy cheek. She lifted her hand to her own breast, then buried her head back into the mattress and sobbed.

David lifted his hands from her waist to her shoulders. The long hand of the clock advanced three more paces.

MaryAnne raised her head and stared at Andrea, memorizing the delicate features of her face, the gentle contour of her florid cheeks, the smooth slope of her chin. Suddenly, the grandfather's clock struck eleven and the hammer rose and fell for an eternity, dividing the moment into agonizing compartments, as if challenging the fragile life to survive the day.

"Stop it. Please, David. Stop it."

David rose and walked to the clock. He opened its case and grasped the brass pendulum, ceasing its motion, then returned to his wife's side as the metallic echo of the chime died, leaving the room in an un-earthly solitude.

MaryAnne suddenly leaned close to Andrea's ear. "I cannot keep you any longer, my love." She swallowed. "I will miss you so." She paused, wiping tears from her cheeks that were as quickly replaced. "Remember me, my love. Remember my love." She laid a hand against the velvet face and bowed her head back into the mattress. "I will remember for both of us."

David pressed the wet flesh of his cheek against MaryAnne's. She swallowed, nuzzled up against the warm, smooth cheek, then, through quivering lips, released her child.

"Go home, my little angel."

As if on command, Andrea suddenly opened her eyes and looked on her mother with no sign of pain or hope, but as one who falls from a cliff might focus their gaze on the ledge they leave behind. Her small chest rose and her lips parted slightly, drawing in breath, struggling against some invisible resistance. Then, in a sudden motion, her eyes turned upward, her tiny body expelled all breath, then no more.

For a moment, all was still. As if all nature had

stopped to recognize the singular fall of a sparrow, until the silence was broken by a single, gasping sob, then another, then the unrestrained flood that poured from MaryAnne's convulsing body. David lifted the quilted cover up over Andrea's face, then pulled Mary-Anne's head against his chest. She would not be comforted.

CHAPTER TEN

The Winter Mourning

"How quickly the fabric of our lives unravels. We weave together protective tapestries of assumption and false belief that are torn to shreds beneath the malevolent claws of reality.

"Grief is a merciless schoolmarm."

DAVID PARKIN'S DIARY. DECEMBER 7, 1913

pon waking, MaryAnne's heart grasped on to the hope that the past few days might only have been a nightmare—then the first moment of recognition was seized by the horrid and breathless remembrance of reality. MaryAnne closed her eyes as the crushing weight of loss constricted her chest in agonizing pain. "No," she moaned.

David took her hand. "MaryAnne."

"I want my baby. Where is my baby?!"

"MaryAnne."

She looked at David through swollen eyes. "No," she moaned. "Where is she?"

"She is gone, my love."

"Bring her back, David. Can't you bring her back?"

David dropped his head in shame, but allowed himself no tears. "No, Mary. I could not even keep her safe."

◆

"In Hebrew, 'Mary' means 'bitter.'"

DAVID PARKIN'S DIARY. DECEMBER 8, 1913

The wagon from the cemetery arrived to bear the small coffin to the knoll—though the casket was small and could have been carried by one man and easily by two.

The noon sun was concealed by a dark tier of clouds as a somber crowd of more than one hundred assembled around the small grave, trampling the snow into a muddy slush.

The jovial greetings of long-unseen friends that usually marked such gatherings had been replaced by simple glances and nods of acknowledgment. Many were there from David's company, whose doors had been closed for the day. The mourners, apparently confused at the etiquette of such an occasion, were not sure how to dress. Some arrived in black and others in stark white.

A fine rain began to fall—a mist at first, which turned into a torrential downpour shortly before the ceremony. Few of the mourners held umbrellas or parasols, as rain in Utah was rare in December. David and MaryAnne stood uncovered, oblivious to the tempest. Mark raised his coat over MaryAnne and held it there the length of the service.

At the head of the cut patch of earth stood the same silver-haired priest who had presided at the wedding of David and MaryAnne four years previous, but his eyes reflected no memory of that happy day. An old man held an umbrella over him, shielding the clergyman from the rain. He raised a white book in his hands and the congregation bowed their heads. His breath froze before him.

"Oh Holy Father, whose blessed Son, in his love for little children, said, 'Suffer little children to come unto me, and forbid them not.' We thank thee for this merciful assurance of thy love, for we believe that thou hast been pleased to take unto thyself the soul of this thy child. Open thou our eyes, we beseech thee, that we may perceive that this child is in the everlasting arms of thine infinite love, and that thou wilt bestow upon her the blessings of thy gracious favor. Amen."

MaryAnne stepped forward and, kneeling, placed a simple white flower on Andrea's casket while David held her shoulders. She quaked as the small wooden box was slowly lowered into the earth's cavity. There was a brief moment of silence before the priest dismissed the proceedings and David helped his wife to her feet. With wordless embraces, the crowd somberly filed past David and MaryAnne to pay their respects, then returned to the forgetful sanctuary of their own homes.

◆

Officer Brookes sauntered into the bar, surrounded by the cold stares of contempt its patrons reserved for lawmen and bill collectors. Brookes was known in the tavern and, though not large of stature, had developed a reputation of being quick of gun and temper.

"Where's Cal Barker?" he shouted over the din. The room quieted, but there was no offer of the man's whereabouts. The officer walked over to a slovenly man nursing a tall brown bottle: Wallace Schoefield.

He looked up at Brookes with a disdainful grin. His teeth were tobacco-stained and one front tooth was cracked sharp from a barroom brawl.

"Where is Barker, Wallace?"

The man leered at the policeman, then turned away, tapping his fingers on the slat counter. There were sudden footsteps behind him. Brookes spun around.

"Looking fer me?" Barker asked coolly.

"You're under arrest, Cal."

"Fer?"

"You know what for."

"Don't know nothin'." His thin lips pursed in a confident grin. "It's my right, ain't it? To know what I've supposed to have done before I'm arrested for doin' it."

"I'm arresting you for arson. And the murder of a child."

Through the corner of his eye, Brookes noticed the surprise on Wallace's face.

"What child?" Wallace asked.

Barker stepped in front of Wallace.

"The fire set at the Parkin estate trapped their three-year-old daughter," Brookes said venomously. "She is dead."

Wallace turned to Barker, who, in turn, glared back at him, then at the officer.

"You can't come in here makin' accusations without proof. We hain't done nothin'. Don't know nothin' about what you're talkin' about."

"You're under arrest," Brookes repeated stolidly.

"I hain't going. Didn't do nuthin'. I have witnesses."

Brookes lifted his gun to the man's chin, his eyes frosted with hate. "That's right, give me any reason, Barker. I have always wanted to kill you anyway."

Barker looked into the man's fierce eyes, scowled, then walked out of the tavern ahead of the officer.

◆

"There is an oft-misunderstood statement: 'Misery loves company.' To some, it implies that the miserable seek to make others like unto themselves. But it is not the meaning, rather there is a universality in grief, a family of sorrow clinging to each other on the brink of the abyss of despair. . . .

" . . . I once heard it preached that pain is the currency of salvation. If it is so, surely we have bought heaven."

DAVID PARKIN'S DIARY. DECEMBER 17, 1913

Dark stratus clouds hung low and flat across the horizon in a gray, mournful pall. The naked and snow-gripped branches of the back estate bent in a frayed canopy to frame the barren winter landscape. Even the sentinel evergreens seemed shaded in a toneless, dusty hue.

The roof of the gazebo lay shrouded beneath thick snow and the dead vines of rose bushes intertwined through the latticework of the structure, frozen and coated in ice. MaryAnne, cloaked in a heavy black bombazine shawl, sat motionless on the suspended swing as still as the clinging icicles that encircled her.

Catherine wrapped herself in a heavy wool shawl and followed MaryAnne's path to the gazebo. She kicked the snow from her pointed, high-laced leather boots and sat down next to MaryAnne on the still bench, breathing the frigid air that froze the nostrils as well as the exhalation. The two women sat at length in silence. Finally, Catherine looked over.

"Are you warm enough, MaryAnne?"

MaryAnne diverted her gaze and nodded. Catherine looked ahead into the unending horizon of white, sniffed, then rubbed her nose. "I have tried to reason what to say that might be of comfort," she said, her voice weak from emotion. "It is too lofty an ambition for words." She fell silent again.

A solitary magpie lit on an ice-caked sundial, cried

out into the gray winter air, then flew back into its cold grasp.

MaryAnne's eyes stared vacantly ahead.

"I have done the same," she said softly. "I tell myself that she will live in my memory. There should be comfort in this." She wiped her reddened eyes with her sleeve. "I should not say 'live.' 'Embalmed' is a better word. Each memory embalmed and dressed in grave clothes with a headstone marking the time and place as a reminder that I will never see my Andrea again."

Catherine said nothing, but looked somberly on, her eyes moistened with her friend's pain.

"There are things I do not understand about my pain, Catherine. If I had to choose never to have known Andrea or to have known her for one brief moment, I would have chosen to have known her and considered myself fortunate. Is it the unexpectedness that causes my grief?"

Catherine pulled her shawl up high enough to cover her chin. "How is David?"

MaryAnne swallowed. "I do not know how David feels, he says nothing. But I see the gray in his eyes and it frightens me. It is the gray of hate, not grief." She shook her head. "It is not just Andrea's life that was taken from us."

There was a moment of silence, then MaryAnne suddenly erupted in rage.

"Listen to me, Catherine! Our lives! My memories! My pain! It is all so selfish! One would think that it is I who had died! Am I so consumed with myself and my own agony that I do not even know if I am mourning for what my little girl has lost . . ." She stopped, her mouth quivering beyond her ability to speak, and lifted a hand to her face. "Or . . . or what I have lost?"

Catherine closed her eyes tightly.

"The wretched fool that I am. Such a selfish, piti-ful . . ."

Catherine grabbed MaryAnne's shoulders and pulled her into her arms. Tears streaked down both women's cheeks. "MaryAnne, no! Do not speak such! In what have you done wrong? Did not the mother of our Lord weep at the foot of his cross?!" Catherine pulled MaryAnne's head into her breast and bowed over her, kissing the crown of her head. She wept as MaryAnne sobbed helplessly.

"Oh, Catherine, my arms feel so empty."

◆

*"Such darkness besets me. I crave MaryAnne's laughter al-
most as the drunkard craves his bottle. And for much the
same reasons."*

DAVID PARKIN'S DIARY. DECEMBER 19, 1913

An hour before sunset, Officer Brookes knocked with
the back of his hand on the engraved glass of the front
door of the Parkin home. Catherine greeted him.

"Hello, Officer Brookes."

"Miss Catherine." He removed his hat and stepped
into the house. Looking up, he noticed MaryAnne,
who stood on the balcony above the foyer silently
looking down. He turned away from her sad stare.

"I'll get Mr. Parkin," Catherine said without prompt-
ing.

David emerged from the hallway below. His face
was tight and expressionless. He pointed to the parlor
and Brookes preceded him in. Once inside, David shut
the door.

"Did you arrest Barker?"

"Yes, he's in jail. For now," he added.

David looked at him quizzically. The officer rubbed

his chin. "I am convinced that it was Barker and his men who set the fire, but there is no proof. There are no witnesses to the crime. At least none who will admit it. Barker has a half-dozen witnesses who claim that he and Wallace were playing cards at the time the fire was set."

David fell silent for a moment as he digested the message. He leaned back against a cabinet.

"One thing more. Your Negro friend was severely beaten that same night—a couple of hours before the fire. Whoever did it left him for dead."

David's jaw clenched in indignation. "Where is Lawrence?"

"He's being cared for at that colored hotel on Second South. His face was swollen and it was difficult for him to speak, but he said something about a gold timepiece being taken. The one that belonged to Hatt's aunt."

Brookes walked across the room and looked out the window into the crimson twilight. "We've got Barker in jail, but we are going to have to release him."

"Can Lawrence identify who beat him?"

"The men were wearing hoods. But even if we could

prove it was Barker and his friends, it still doesn't connect them to your fire. If someone don't come forward, there is nothing we can do."

David felt a sickening rage blacken his mind. "There is always something that can be done," he said half to himself.

A look of grave concern bent the policeman's brow. "I know you must feel the temptation real bad, Mr. Parkin, but don't you go taking matters into your own hands. Your wife needs you. It won't do anyone any good." The officer replaced his hat. "I'm sorry. I'll let you know if something happens. You never know. . . ." He walked to the doorway, then paused and looked back at David with a somber countenance. "Don't go doing something to make me have to arrest you. The injustice of this is already enough to make me vomit."

When he had seen him off, David returned to the room and pulled a Winchester carbine from his gun cabinet. He took a pouch from the shelf below and slid two bullets into its chamber. MaryAnne suddenly appeared in the doorway.

"David?"

He turned toward her.

"What did he say?"

"He said there is nothing they can do. . . ."

MaryAnne quietly looked down, cradling her forehead in her hands, then looked back up at David. "What are you doing?"

His eyes were granite. "What needs to be done."

MaryAnne walked over next to him. "David?"

He would not look at her.

MaryAnne knelt down before him and wrapped her arms around his legs and began to cry. A minute later, she looked up, her eyes filled with pleading.

"They killed our daughter," he said coldly.

"The men who killed our little girl were full of hate and vengeance and sickness. Will we become as they?"

David paused for a moment, then looked down at his wife.

"It is the price of justice."

"Such a price, David! How much more must we pay?!" She took a deep breath, her chin quivered. "Haven't we paid enough already?"

"You would have me forget what they have done?"

MaryAnne gasped. "How could we forget what they have done? We can never forget." She raised her head and as she did their eyes met. "But we can forgive. We must forgive. It is all that we have left of her."

"Forgive?" David asked softly. He broke her grasp and walked to the other side of the room. "Forgive?!" he shouted incredulously. "They murdered our daughter!"

MaryAnne sobbed into her hands, then, without looking up, spoke in a voice feeble with grief. "If this is life, exchanging hate for hate, it is not worth living. Vengeance will not bring her back to us. Forgiveness has nothing to do with them, David. It has to do with us. It has to do with who we are and who we will become." She looked up, her eyes drowned in tears. "It has to do with how we want to remember our daughter."

Her words trailed off in a pleading silence. David stared at his wife. "Who we will become," he repeated softly. He leaned the rifle against the cabinet, then returned and knelt by MaryAnne, wrapping his arms around her as she wept into his chest.

"David, I cannot imagine feeling any joy again in this life. It seems that all I can do is to ride the tide of the day's events. But I cannot bear to see any more hate. We must let it end here." She wiped her eyes with the palm of her hand. "I have already lost one of you to hate."

She placed her hand on his sleeve, gripping it tightly. David looked back over at the gun and as he did, she released her grasp. Her voice became soft, yet deliberate. "I cannot choose for you, David. It is your choice, not mine. But if you will be taken by it, I ask that you promise me just one thing."

David looked into her eyes. They were red and swollen, but beautiful still.

"What would you have me promise, Mary?"

"That you will save one bullet for my heart."

CHAPTER ELEVEN

The Seraph and the Timepiece

"As a child, to visualize nobility was to conjure up images of kings and queens adorned in the majestic, scarlet robes of royalty. As a man, softened by the tutelage of life and time, I have learned a great truth—that true nobility is usually a silent and lonely affair, unaccompanied by the trumpeted fanfare of acclaim. And more times than not, it wears rags."

DAVID PARKIN'S DIARY. DECEMBER 19, 1913

A decrepit, wood-planked wagon drawn by a seasoned mule plodded up the cobblestone drive to the Parkin home. When it neared the double-door entry, Lawrence tied back the reins and climbed down from the buckboard. David had seen the approaching wagon from an upstairs window and descended the stairs to meet it. When he reached the front doorway, Lawrence was already standing on the porch. His forehead was bandaged with white linen strips, and his right eye was nearly swollen shut. His left arm was suspended in a sling. He had removed his hat, and was holding it in his right hand over his chest. His eyes were moist.

"I'm sorry 'bout your little Andrea," he said solemnly.

David lowered his head. Both men were silent.

In the bed of the wagon, a canvas sheet concealed an awkward form. Lawrence wiped his eyes.

"I wanted to do somethin'. I want your Andrea to have my angel."

David said nothing for a moment, then frowned. "No, Lawrence. We couldn't."

"No use, David . . . I gave her up. Thought over it all night. Wha's the use havin' people thinkin' I was somethin' important. If I'm in heaven, it won't matter much, angels all 'bout and such. And if I'm burnin' in hell, shore won't bring much satisfaction. If I'm just cold dead I won' know no difference. No use," he said resolutely, "I said my good-byes. That Andrea, now she's somethin' pure. A child should have an angel." Lawrence glanced up the road, toward the cemetery. "I'll be takin' her up to the sexton's. People be goin' to the grave oughta have somethin' special." His voice choked as he wiped his cheek with his shoulder. "Real Italian marble. You tell MaryAnne there's be somethin' special."

David gazed at the man with quiet respect.

"Jus' somethin' I oughta do," he said solemnly. He put his hat back on his head and turned to leave.

"Lawrence."

"Yessuh."

"Thank you."

Lawrence nodded and with one hand pulled himself up into his rig and coaxed the mule toward the cemetery.

◆

"Today, someone, thinking themselves useful, said to me that it must be a relief to have this 'affair' over with. How indelicately we play each other's heartstrings! How willingly I would carry that pain again for but one glance of her angel face! How she nourished me with her innocence. She once confided in me that the trees are her friends. I asked her how she knew this. She said because they often waved to her. How clearly she saw things! To have such eyes! The trees, for her, shall ever wave to me.

"If I am ever to comfort someone, I will not try to palliate their suffering through foolish reasoning. I will just embrace them and tell them I am heartfelt sorry for their loss."

DAVID PARKIN'S DIARY. DECEMBER 29, 1913

◆

"What prudery so ritualizes my grief as to press my letters with black sealing wax."

DAVID PARKIN'S DIARY. DECEMBER 31, 1913

As the last six hours of the waning year fell beneath the tireless sweep of the grandfather's clock's serpentine hands, Catherine found David in the drawing room sitting at the marble-topped writing nook, barefoot and dressed only in nightclothes and a crimson robe. He wrote with a quill pen, and a crystal well of India ink sat at the head of the stationery. In the background a wide-mouthed Victrola scratched out a Caruso solo of *La Forza del Destino*.

"Sir?"

David looked up from his letter. "Yes, Catherine."

"Officer Brookes is come."

David lifted a corner of the letter and blew the ink. "I will see him."

"I will let him know." She quickly stepped away. David set down the pen, tightening the sash on his robe, as he left the room. Brookes was not in the foyer as he expected but stood outside the home, twenty feet from the doorway. He had declined Catherine's invitation to enter. Just as peculiar, the police wagon was parked in the shadow of the home's gated entrance and Brookes had walked the length of the drive to the house. David walked out. He found the scene odd and the strange expression on the lawman's face offered no explanation.

"Last night Wallace Schoefield shot himself through the head," Brookes said bluntly.

David stared ahead coldly. He could not pretend sympathy.

"He couldn't live with what they'd done. Barker wanted you, and Wallace and four others went along with him. He said they didn't know about the child."

David looked past the officer toward his horse-drawn paddy wagon. "Who did he tell?"

"He left a letter. Barker started the fire by leaving a bottle of kerosene around the back of your home with gunpowder and a cigar to ignite it after they had left. That's why Barker wasn't there when the fire started."

Behind him, the horse whinnied and shook its head impatiently.

"The child was killed unintentionally." Officer Brookes suddenly squinted, then removed his revolver from his holster and handed it to David, who looked up quizzically. Brookes's eyes darted back and forth nervously. His voice dropped coldly.

"They'll send Barker to prison, but they won't be hanging him. He's getting off easy. He should die for what he's done. Barker's locked in the wagon. If you want to kill him, I'll say that I shot him in the taking."

David caressed the gun in his hand. It was evenly balanced and he ran his fingertips along the engraving that rose up its steel barrel. He stared at it for a moment, rubbed his forehead, then handed the gun back to the officer.

"No," he said softly. He turned and began to walk away.

The response surprised Brookes, who returned the firearm to its holster. "It's better than he deserves," he shouted after him.

David stopped and looked at the officer. "Yea. It probably is. But it is not better than Andrea deserves." He looked back at the wagon and frowned. "Do your duty, Officer."

The officer tipped his hat. "Good evening, Mr. Parkin. To a new year."

"Good evening, Brookes."

◆

At Catherine's summons, MaryAnne came to David in the drawing room. She found him gazing silently out the tall twelve-paned windows that lined the north wall. She paused at the doorway, then slowly entered.

"David?"

He turned around. He was still wearing his robe and was unshaven, with several days' growth shading his lower face. His eyes were red-rimmed. For a brief moment, she felt a pang of apprehension, as though she were approaching a stranger, not her beloved.

"Remember, Mary? This is where we met our guests at our wedding. It looks so different to me now." He surveyed the surroundings as if the room held some new intrigue. "Of course, there were flowers . . . and that palm . . ."

MaryAnne clasped her hands behind her back. His words seemed to float with no apparent destination. She suddenly felt afraid.

"I am sorry. I am babbling like an idiot." He ran a

hand through his hair, then breathed heavily. He turned back toward her. "I do not know how I am to act, MaryAnne. How a man is to act."

MaryAnne stared back quietly.

"I walk around with this stone expression like some kind of statue. But I do not have a stone heart." His eyes moistened. "And I wonder if this wall I have built up is to protect me from further assault or to retain the last vestige of humanity within me. Are men not supposed to feel loss? Because I feel it, Mary. I feel it as heavy as a horse falling on me." He lowered his head. "And I miss my little girl and I don't even feel worthy to do so."

His voice began to crack.

"She was so small and needed someone to protect her." He raised a hand to his chest. "I was to protect her, Mary. Every instinct I was born with cries out that I must protect her!" His voice rose in an angry crescendo, then fell sharply in a despairing monotone. "And I failed. I have more than failed, I have caused her death." A tear fell down his cheek. His lips quivered.

"Oh, what I would give to hold her just once more. To hear her forgive me for failing her." He wiped his cheek, then lowered his head. MaryAnne walked across the room to him, then stopped abruptly. On the counter beside him lay two bullets. She looked up for an explanation. David glanced at the bullets, then back up into her face.

"You were right. It is all that I have left of her. All my feelings and love for Andrea were in my heart—" he rubbed his eyes—"and hate kills the heart. Even broken ones."

He took a deep breath, then, in anguish, dropped his head in his hands and began to weep. "I need you, Mary. I need you."

MaryAnne took him in her arms, then pulled his head to her breast as he fell to his knees and, for the first time since Andrea's death, wept uncontrollably.

◆

Five years later. Salt Lake City, 1918

"There are moments, it would seem, that were created in cosmic theater where we are given strange and fantastic tests. In these times, we do not show who we are to God, for surely He must already know, but rather to ourselves."

DAVID PARKIN'S DIARY. DECEMBER 8, 1918

It was a chill night and the winter winds rolled in frozen gusts down the foothills of the Wasatch Range, drawing the valley in its crystalline breath. Two hours after the sun had fallen, a child, not suitably clad for such a December night, knocked on the front door of the Parkin home.

David was out of the state on business and as Catherine had been given leave for the evening, MaryAnne came to the foyer to greet the winter visitor. As she opened the door, a chill ran up her spine. MaryAnne recognized the girl right away. She was the daughter of Cal Barker.

"What brings you here, child?" MaryAnne asked softly.

The little girl timidly raised her head. Her face was gaunt and her clothes were dirty and ill fit.

"I would like some food, ma'am," she replied humbly. Her breath froze before her.

MaryAnne stared for a moment, then slowly stepped away from the door. "Come in."

The girl stepped into the house. Her eyes were filled with wonder at its richness and beauty. MaryAnne led her down the corridor, then into the dining room, where she pulled a chair away from the table.

"Sit down," she said.

The girl obeyed, dwarfed by the ornate, high-backed chair. MaryAnne left the room, then returned a few moments later with a plate of bread and curd cheese, a sliced pear, and a small bowl of broth. She watched in silence as the girl devoured the meal. When she had finished eating, the child leaned back from the table and looked around the room. Her eyes focused on a small gold-framed photograph of Andrea, clothed in a beautiful umber velvet dress with a lace-bibbed bodice. She smiled at MaryAnne.

"You have a little girl!"

MaryAnne stared at the child, then slowly shook her head. "No. Not anymore."

"Where is she?" The girl's brown eyes blinked quizzically, partially covered by the long, dirty strands that fell over her face. "She would be lucky to live in this house."

MaryAnne looked down at the Persian rug and blinked away the pooling tears. "She is gone. She had to go away." She took a deep breath. "How old are you, child?"

"I am nine years."

MaryAnne looked carefully into her face. She

thought she appeared older than her nine years—aged as a child who has had the harsh realities of life thrust upon her. "What is your name?"

"Martha Ann Barker, ma'am."

MaryAnne stood and walked over to the window. The snow outside fell in scattered showers and in the distance snaked across the paved street in snow-blown skiffs. "My little girl would be nine this winter," MaryAnne said into the frosted windowpanes. She stared out into the black. ". . . This January." She suddenly turned toward her small guest. "It is late for you to be out."

"I was so hungry."

"Haven't your parents any food?"

She shook her head. "My father was in the jail. No one lets him work."

The child's directness surprised her. "Do you know why he was put in jail?"

She shook her head again. "The boys say that he killed a child. I asked my mama, but she just cries, mostly."

MaryAnne nodded her head slowly. "Why did you come here? To this house."

"I saw the fire from the street. It looked so warm and nice inside."

"The fire . . . ," MaryAnne repeated softly. She sat down at the table next to her guest, contemplating the strange circumstance that had befallen her. She had been given a gift. A terrible, wonderful gift. The chance to see her own soul. She sat motionless, her hands joined in her lap, as her mind reeled with emotions. Then a single tear fell down her cheek. The girl observed it curiously. MaryAnne leaned close to the child and took her face in her hands.

"You must remember this night, Martha. You are loved here. You must know this for the rest of your life."

The girl stared back blankly.

"You will understand someday." MaryAnne stood up. "Just a moment, dear." She left the room, then returned with a small bag of flour and a canister of salted bacon, as much as she thought the child could carry. In a kerchief, stowed in the canister, MaryAnne had wrapped three gold coins.

"Can you carry this?"

Martha shook her head. "Yes, ma'am. I am strong."

MaryAnne nodded sadly. "I can see that. Now you run home and take this to your mama." She escorted Martha back out to the foyer and opened the door. A chill wind swept into the house. "Remember, Martha. You are always welcome. You are loved here."

The little girl stepped out the door, walked a few paces, then turned back. "Thank you, ma'am."

"You are welcome, child."

She looked at the woman gratefully. "Don't be sad. Your little girl will come home." The girl smiled innocently, then turned quickly and disappeared into the winter night. MaryAnne shut the door and fell against it weeping.

◆

The next morning, the first sheaths of dawn illuminated the windows of the downstairs parlor in iridescent brilliance, meeting MaryAnne, where it had daily for the past five years, before a fireplace reading her Bible. The Bible David had brought back with a wooden box, a porcelain music box, and an oversized dress that would never be worn. The book bore witness of her devotion to the daily ritual, marred with teardrops and wrinkled pages. MaryAnne had followed the routine every morning since she had lost Andrea, holding to the words as one who is drowning seizes a life ring.

At the conclusion of her reading, MaryAnne wiped her eyes, then replaced the Gothic book on the elaborately carved rosewood bookshelf. She donned her coat and scarf and started outside on her daily trek to the angel statue.

The winter air was damp and heavy, carrying moisture pilfered from the Great Salt Lake, which salt-saturated consistency kept it from freezing even in the severest of winters.

In the distance, MaryAnne could see the angel at the top of a knoll, its head and wings capped in a new-fallen shroud of snow. She walked solemnly, her head bowed. She need not look to find her way, she could have followed the trail without sight.

She suddenly stopped.

In the freshly fallen snow were tracks leading to the angel. Heavy tracks, clumsy, large-bodied footprints that had come, and departed, falling back on themselves, but leaving evidence of the visitor at the base of the grave. MaryAnne approached pensively. Someone, that very morning, had knelt at the foot of the angel.

As she neared, she could see that the snow had been

wiped from the stone pedestal. On its surface, she saw a small parcel, a white flour sack bundle bound with jute. She looked around her. The morning sun illuminated the grounds and the snow sparkled in a virgin, crystalline blanket. All was still and quiet and alone.

Noiselessly, she stooped down and lifted the offering. As she pulled back the cloth, the contents cast a gold reflection on the surrounding coarse material—a soft radiance from the treasure that lay within. There, without a note, on the marble step of the monument, had been laid a rose-gold timepiece.

XII

CHAPTER TWELVE

The Endowment

Salt Lake City, 1967

stood outside Jenna's room holding the velveteen case in my hands. My throat was dry as I slid the box into my trouser pocket and knocked gently on the door. A soft voice answered.

"Come in."

I stepped into the room. Jenna sat on her bed writing in her diary. A bridal gown, sheathed in a transparent garment bag, hung from the closet door above a new pair of boxed white satin pumps.

"Hi, sweetheart."

Her face wore the unique blend of melancholy and excitement given rise on such an occasion. I sat down on the bed next to her.

"Are you ready for tomorrow?"

Jenna shrugged. "I don't think I will ever be ready."

"I was just thinking the same about myself," I said. "I once read a poem about the pain of a father sending his daughter to another village to be married. It was written four thousand years ago in China. Maybe things never really change."

Jenna bowed her head.

"I just remind myself that this is what I've always hoped for you. All I have ever wanted for you is to be happy."

She leaned over and hugged me.

"I have something I need to give you." I brought the box from my pocket and set it in her hands. Her eyes shone with delight as she opened the case.

"It's beautiful." She lifted the delicate timepiece from the case, dangling it admiringly from one end. "Thank you."

"It's not from me," I said. "But it is from someone who loved you very much." Jenna looked at me quizzically.

"It's from MaryAnne."

My words sounded strange even to me—a name on a grave near the stone angel we visited every Christmas, now resurrected in a single act of giving.

"MaryAnne," she repeated. She looked up into my

eyes. "I don't really remember her," Jenna said sadly. "Not really. I remember her once holding me in a chair and reading to me. How good I felt around her."

"Then you remember her, Jenna. She loved you as if you were her own. In some ways, you were."

Jenna looked back down at the timepiece.

"Nineteen years ago, MaryAnne asked me to give this to you the night before your wedding. It was her most prized possession."

Jenna shook her head in astonishment. "She wanted me to have it?"

I nodded. "MaryAnne was a good giver of gifts," I said.

She draped the gold watch back in its case, set it on her nightstand, then sighed. "So are you, Dad."

I smiled.

"Dad?"

"Yes?"

She turned away and I noticed that her chin quivered as she struggled to speak. As she turned back, her tear-filled eyes met mine. "So, how do you thank someone for a life?"

I wiped a tear from my cheek as I stared back into

my daughter's beautiful eyes. Then, in that bittersweet moment, I understood MaryAnne's words of the gift. The great gift. The meaning of the timepiece.

"You give it back, Jenna. You give it back." I took my girl in my arms and held her tightly to my chest. My heart, bathed in fond memory, ached in the sweet pain of separation. This is what it meant to be a father—had always meant. To know that one day I would turn around and my little girl would be gone. Finally, reluctantly, I released her and leaned back, looking down into her angelic face. It was time. Time for the cycle to begin anew.

"It's late, sweetheart. You have a big day tomorrow." I leaned over and kissed her tenderly on the cheek. "Good-bye, honey."

It was good-bye. To an era. A time never to be returned to. Her eyes shone with sadness and love. "Good-bye, Daddy."

The silence of the snow-shrouded evening enveloped the moment and time seemed to stand still for just a moment. For just us.

I took a deep breath, rose from the side of her bed, and with one last embrace walked from her room. I descended the stairway with a new lightness of understanding. I understood what MaryAnne had meant by the gift. The gift Jenna had given me had been life. That the very breath I had once given to her had come back to me in an infinite return of joy and life and meaning.

In the dimly lit entrance below, the grandfather's clock struck once for the hour, and I paused momentarily at the base of the stairway to look into its time-faded face as, perhaps, MaryAnne and David had done so many years before.

This relic will outlive us all, I thought, just as it had outlived generations before us. For within its cotillion of levers and cogs and gears, there was still time. Time to outlive all things human. Yet, in my heart, something told me otherwise. For perhaps there was some quality about love that sprang eternal—that a love like MaryAnne's, and like mine, could last forever.

Not could. Would. This was the message of the timepiece. To let go of this world and aspire to something far nobler in a realm that regards no boundaries of time.

I glanced back upstairs as the light switched off in my little girl's room and I smiled. Twenty years after MaryAnne's death, she had bestowed upon me one last gift of understanding. I wondered if, in some unseen realm, MaryAnne was watching and was pleased that I had learned her lesson. That some things, like a parent's love, do last forever in a time and place where all broken hearts will forever be made whole. And if, in the silent vastness of a mysterious universe, or in the quietness of men's hearts, there is such a place as heaven, then it couldn't be anything more than that.

Richard Paul Evans is the bestselling author of *The Christmas Box*. He lives in Salt Lake City, Utah, with his wife, Keri, and their three daughters, Jenna, Allyson, and Abigail. He is currently working on his next novel.